Superb Writing
to Fire the Imagination

Catherine Fisher writes, 'The oldest stories are often the best. And the story of someone – in this case a Victorian girl – who sells her soul to an immortal power and lives to regret the bargain, has to be one of the oldest in the world. I have been fascinated by the possibilities of it for some time. I've also become interested in alchemy, and I hope the two make a potent mixture. Darkwater Hall is an image of the power and knowledge we all desire. But what will we pay for them, and are they worth the price?'

Her first published novel, *The Conjurer's Game*, was shortlisted for the Smarties Book Prize, and *The Candle Man*, set on the eerie Gwent Levels, won the Tir Na n-Og prize. Her acclaimed fantasy series *The Snow-Walker's Son* was shortlisted for the W. H. Smith Mind Boggling Books Award. Catherine's latest books include *The Lammas Field* and the ongoing *Book of the Crow* fantasies. Jan Mark wrote of *The Lammas Field* in the *T.E.S.*: 'This is strong, passionate writing, deep and quite unsettling . . .'

Darkwater Hall

CATHERINE FISHER

**Hodder
Children's
Books**

A division of Hodder Headline Limited

A Catalogue record for this book is available from
the British Library

ISBN 0 340 74383 2

Typeset by Avon Dataset Ltd, Bidford-on-Avon, Warks

Printed and bound in Great Britain by
The Guernsey Press Co. Ltd, Channel Isles

Hodder Children's Books
A Division of Hodder Headline Limited
338 Euston Road
London NW1 3BH

'The angel of the Covenant you are longing for, yes he is coming, says the Lord.
Who will be able to resist the day of his coming?
Who will be able to stand before him?
For he is like the refiner's fire and the fuller's alkali.
He will purify the sons of Levi and refine them like gold . . .'

BOOK OF MALACHI

THE PRINCE OF DARKNESS

ONE

In the dream, she hurried down an endless corridor lined with books. Shelf on shelf they towered over her head, leaning out, frowning down, disapproving. She knew they wanted to fall on her and crush her.

Nervous, she walked faster, wishing she had a ladder so she could climb up to them, the thousands of heavy volumes, the folios, encyclopaedias, vast flat atlases, thin slivers of poetry. There were books bound in vellum and calfskin, unicorn and dragon skin, some still with wings and sleepy eyes that blinked at her; fastened and locked with clasps and huge keys and chains that encircled them like prisoners. Fat bibles, expensively crusted with gold, filled a whole shelf, their cameos of dead emperors high and dim and sneering. All out of reach.

Uneasy, she tiptoed now. Even a breath would make them topple, a whisper set off an avalanche of pages, crashing spines.

Then she stopped.

She had come to a thin mirror, squeezed between shelves, and it showed her own sudden reflection. In the grimy glass she was wearing a rich girl's clothes. A blue dress, ruched and glinting with pearls. Her hair was clean and brushed: on her feet wonderfully frail ivory slippers.

Astonished, she stared at herself. A cat came out of the shadows and sat there, eyes bright.

'What do you think of this?' she said to it. 'I'm a lady.'

She turned, gathering handfuls of the skirt. It was silk, fine and delicate, but as she touched it it withered and shrivelled until she held only cobwebs, fistfuls of sticky, filthy dust.

Something crashed past her shoulder.

She jerked back, heart pounding.

A book had fallen.

It lay there in the dust. She crouched and opened it, her knees breaking through the disintegrating dress. It was clasped with great hinges like a gate; creaking it wide she read one enormous word.

ALCHEMIE

Then, in curly letters underneath,

Being the Arte of Transmuting Base and useless
Metal into Gold

The page was dusted with gold. It came off on her fingers and her hands were shining with it, but before she could turn over another book crashed, and then more, a whole stack wobbling and thundering behind her, sending echoes and dust flying into her eyes. The corridor rang with vibrations; all the precarious heaps above her quivering.

And in the mirror, quite suddenly, she saw a boy watching her. He was faint and strange through the grime, and he separated into a double image, so that there were two of him. Then he put his hand out through the glass and caught hold of hers.

She screeched.

6

'Sarah!'

Martha was shaking her hard. 'For mercy's sake! It's seven o'clock!'

Sarah sat up, quickly. Sweat was cold on her. Through the rag nailed over the window a grey light gleamed. 'What?' she mumbled.

'You're late! You know what she said! This morning of all mornings!' Martha hurried out. 'You won't have time to eat a morsel.'

Shivering, the dream dissolved in seconds, Sarah scrambled out of the truckle bed. Her clothes were flung over a chair; she dragged them on; the harsh grey skirt, the jacket that used to be Martha's son's, the patched shawl. Forcing her feet into icy boots she laced them desperately, dragged the curtain wide and ran into the dark kitchen, where Martha pushed a crust and a comb into her hands, holding the baby expertly on her hip.

'You'll lose this situation, my girl.'

'I wish I could.' Sarah dragged the comb through her hair. 'I could earn more in the workhouse,' she said, pin between teeth.

'Aye. And learn less.'

'I don't get to learn much. And I hate that woman.'

'There's worse,' Martha said darkly. 'Besides, it would kill your father. The last of the Trevelyans in a dame school is one thing. In the workhouse is another.' Taking the comb back she said quietly, 'He's been awake a while.'

Sarah paused, reluctant. Then she went through the door in the corner.

Her father's room was always dim. He lay on his side, facing away from her, as if that helped him to breathe. When he turned, his face was clammy and pale, his hair whiter than the pillow.

'Oh it's you,' he said.

'I'm off to work.'

'Is it today?' he wheezed.

She cursed herself for telling him. He'd probably been brooding on it all night.

'Is what?'

'You know what.' He struggled to sit up; she had to pull the thin bolster up behind him. 'All the grand visitors. All the lords and ladies. Coming to inspect you, look down their noses at you.'

Sarcasm made him cough. She poured the medicine hastily into the blue cup and helped him drink it. When he lay back she said, 'They won't look at me. I'm no one. And I'm late.'

'Mind you take no nonsense. They'll know you. If your grandfather hadn't gambled it all away, we'd be the ones being bowed and scraped to, inspecting schools, giving prizes, my lord this, my lady that.'

'Yes, I know,' she said impatiently. He was back on the old subject, the old grievance. It haunted him, always. She edged away.

'It's money, Sarah. That's all they've got. You've got family. A pedigree going back to the Norman kings. They can't say that. Not that fat mayor or that interfering old bag from the Grange . . .'

'Lie still, Papa,' she muttered. 'I've got to go.'

As she reached the door he caught his breath. Blue at the lips he gasped, 'I suppose he'll be there.'

'Who?'

'That stinking upstart. The one who stole our house.'

All down the lane she cursed herself with irritated names. It was bad enough that she had to skivvy for Old Mother Hubbard in her paltry little school without him imagining all the gentry of the parish gossiping about her.

'That's Sarah Trevelyan.'

'Not THE Trevelyans?'

'The ones who lost all their money.'

'The ones who lost Darkwater Hall.'

It was late. She ran, round the corner and into the stone-walled lane that trickled down to the sea, a squall of salty rain slapping her in the face. Leaping every puddle she climbed the stile and squelched over Martinmas Field, the sheep scattering with low bleats. On the far side the wall had slipped and she paused on the wobbling stones at the top to catch breath.

And saw what she saw every morning.

Darkwater Hall rose on the clifftop of High Bluff. Turreted and bleak, its facade of gothic windows caught the blear light and gleamed, facing out to sea. Down its roofs and gables the rain ran in sheets, and the peculiarly grotesque gargoyles that her great-grandfather had insisted on in his eccentric plan spat and grinned evilly into the tangle of gardens below.

From here, she could just see the main door. Outside it a carriage had pulled up; a sleek, black equipage with two grey horses, each blinkered. They pawed the ground restlessly, and as she watched a hunched footman came down from the house and opened the carriage door.

She watched, intent.

The house – their house – had long been empty. Lord Azrael had arrived suddenly, last week. Martha had gossiped about it to Jack, always stopping when Sarah came in. How her father had found out she didn't know.

A man came down the steps. She was surprised; she'd expected someone old; withered and ugly. But this man was young, dark haired with a neat, barely visible clipped beard. He walked with a limp, and his frockcoat looked expensive. At the top of the steps he paused.

Then he turned and looked up.

She ducked, wobbling.

The dark man didn't move. Ignoring the horses and the impatient footman he stared out across the fields, the wind blowing his hair. As if he knew someone was watching him.

Sarah shivered. Rain ran down her neck. For a second she felt as if she was balancing not on a wall but on the edge of some terrible pit, and if she moved she would plummet, head over heels into darkness.

Then the new owner of Darkwater turned and went inside.

The giddyness passed. The stones slewed sideways. She jumped, splashed puddle water up her stocking, and ran. In the distance a cracked bell was clanking relentlessly.

By the time she got to the school she was breathless, the crust jammed unnoticed in her pocket, her left foot soaked from a leak in her boot. Praying they hadn't gone in yet she tore round the great oak tree and flung herself in at the gate.

The courtyard was empty.

'Blast!' she hissed.

TWO

She turned the knob quietly.

Inside the tiny porch shawls and caps dripped. Immediately the smell of the place enfolded her, and she frowned. She hated this smell. Damp clothes, smoke, polish, sweat. And fear.

She creaked the door open and went in.

'So! You've finally decided to arrive!' Mrs Hubbard was squeezed into the pulpit of her desk, a dark ominous whale of a woman, pinned and brooched into a vast starched gown of bombazine black. Her best, Sarah realized.

'I'm sorry,' she said, tightly. 'My father . . .'

'Your father is a convenient excuse too frequently employed.' Mrs Hubbard raised a magnificent lorgnette which magnified her small black eyes and looked Sarah up and down in distaste. 'Dear me. You could have made more effort in your dress. I wasn't expecting flounces and bows but even a family as horridly reduced as yours should have managed better. You're a disgrace, dearie. What are you?'

'A disgrace,' Sarah muttered automatically.

'This is an important day for me.' Mrs Hubbard stabbed a pointing fingernail at the class; they seemed to huddle down further without even seeing it. 'My establishment is noted, noted, mind you, for its discipline. On the day when my patrons inspect it you turn up

11

looking like a workhouse brat. There are plenty of others who could have this situation.' She opened her desk, took a pinch of snuff and sniffed it, daintily. 'I ain't too fussy, dear, about who cleans the privies. Now. Stove first. Then sweep.'

Sarah turned and went for the bucket in silent relief. Old Mother Hubbard must be preoccupied. Otherwise the tirade would have gone on and on.

Above the smeared mirror next to the world map a notice said CLEAN HANDS REVEAL A CLEAN HEART in smug letters. She ignored them and brushed wisps of her hair hastily back, seeing her red face, chapped from the wind. In the back row Elsie Tate gave her a spiteful glance. Elsie was one of the favoured pupils; her mother paid extra fees for her little darling to learn deportment and dancing. Watching her stagger round on Thursday afternoons with a pile of books on her head, Sarah thought grimly, was almost worth all the rest.

The dame school was one dingy room. Tilted ranks of ancient tables descended in three tiers to an open space where Mrs Hubbard's pulpit rose like a tower. The desk had a power of its own. Even when she tottered down from it – which was rare – it cast its dark shadow of fear. The class were terrorized by its silence.

The front row was six tiny boys and an even tinier girl, who never spoke. Today she was crying again, Sarah noticed, the tears hurriedly mopped into her sleeve before they touched the precious slate. No one took any notice.

'Class.' Mrs Hubbard polished her lorgnette in gloved fingers. 'Gibbon. From yesterday. Begin.'

Hands reached for chalk. The morning exercise was

12

always the same – the painstaking copying of Gibbon's *Rise and Fall of the Roman Empire* – probably the only book on the shelf, Sarah thought sourly, that the old bag ever bothered to open. The children's chilblained fingers made careful copperplate on the slates, the older few in the back dipping pens into tiny inkpots, in agonies not to blot the cheap yellow paper.

Sarah didn't have time to watch. The room was bitterly cold; she took the bucket out and filled it with coal, picking the largest pieces out of the filthy heap next to the privies. Soon her hands were black; she pushed her hair back and felt the smudge of soot down her face.

Back inside she stoked the small stove and lit it; it was carefully placed to face the pulpit, so no one else got much benefit. Every tiny scrabble of noise she made seemed huge; the room was a deep well of silence.

Next she swept, the coarse scraping of the bristles raising a cloud of dust that hung in the air, so that a boy coughed and Mrs Hubbard's glare nailed him like an owl on a mouse.

'Do that again luvvie and I'll mark your card. You're a dolt. What are you?'

'A dolt,' the boy breathed, in terror.

Mrs Hubbard smiled. She raised her desk lid, poured a tot of gin into a tiny glass and drank it. Her fingers mopped daintily at her lips.

It was a terrible morning. The tension in the room grew as the clock ticked on, ominous as the grey thunderclouds that gathered outside. Gulls cried over the roof; Mrs Hubbard glowered up as if she wanted to dismiss them on the spot. She was tetchy and irritable and more and more coldly humorous as twelve o'clock came nearer. Her fingers tapped a drum roll of impatience on the desk, so that a few of the younger ones glanced up and were caught, staring hypnotised with dread. And always she was listening, her small eyes darting to the door.

Sarah was working grimly. Every corner of the paintwork had to be wiped; colonies of spiders and woodlice eliminated without fuss. She had to arrange the books, dust the pictures of Queen Victoria, Albert and Gladstone, straighten the world map, give out supplies of beautifully new pens and pencils that would only be used for the duration of the governors' visit. Mrs Hubbard kept these in a box and used the same ones every year. Finally, the privies had to be cleaned; a stinking job Sarah loathed, but at least she was out of the stifling schoolroom.

Emptying the bucket she paused a moment, leaning against the stone wall, letting the wind touch her face, salty from the sea. She despised and hated the school. At least, the way it was now. It might have been a happy place, with real learning; if she stayed on long enough she might become the teacher herself. But the thought of years of this turned her cold. It was only the books that kept her here.

There was a small shelf of them over the old mantelpiece. Mrs Hubbard never looked at them, but on Friday nights after everyone had gone and she had scrubbed the floor, Sarah read them. Mr Dicken's novels, and Jane Austen's and a book about old Greek gods and a great battle at Troy that lasted ten years. And there were two histories too, all about the Normans and Stuarts and Tudors, that really told you about them, not like Mrs

Hubbard who insisted on nothing but dates and names. There was an atlas with maps of utterly strange places; the Hindu Kush, Rhodesia, Paris. And above all there was half an encyclopaedia, A to M, with satisfying articles on how steam is made from coal, and how animals see in the dark. She had read them all, and was beginning again from this week. That was knowledge, she thought. Real learning. She wanted more of it. If she had money she'd buy books of her own, but that was a hopeless dream. Like the library at Darkwater Hall.

A gull screamed a warning. She scowled, and went back in.

The class were chanting tables in a breathless gabble.

Mrs Hubbard snapped, 'Enough.'

Her black eyes watched them as Sarah gathered up the slates, hastily. The classroom was a semi-circle of fear, the tiny girl at the front rocking with anxiety.

'Stop that!' Mrs Hubbard barked.

The girl froze.

'Any mistakes?'

Sarah scanned the slates quickly. She hated this. If she said yes, someone would suffer. If she said no, she'd suffer.

'No,' she said, glancing up.

'Liar.' Mrs Hubbard said. 'What are you?'

'A liar, Mrs Hubbard.'

'Put them there. I'll look at them myself, later.' The class relaxed a fraction. They knew she wouldn't bother.

'Second row. Monarchs of England. Begin.'

She never used their names. It was as if that would make them people, and she didn't want people. Just dolts, and liars and snivelling scared faces. Sarah backed off to the corner cupboard and stacked the slates inside. The boy – Archie, it was – was chanting in a monotone, careful not to sound too clever, or too slow. Mrs Hubbard listened, half to him and half for the door, turning her snuffbox over and over.

'Enough.' She looked bored.

Archie sat down, instantly.

'Next.'

Reflected in the glass Sarah saw who was next, and winced. It would have to be Emmeline.

Emmeline Rowney was thin. She had something wrong with one of her eyes; it never looked at you straight. She was scrawny and came from a family who could hardly pay the fee; her mother slaved as a washer woman to get enough. Maybe that was why Mrs Hubbard enjoyed Emmeline so much.

The girl stood up, licked her lips and said carefully, 'Edward the Third, Richard the Second, Henry the . . . Fifth, Henry . . .'

Mrs Hubbard jerked upright. She seemed overjoyed. 'What? What did you say?'

Emmeline froze.

'Repeat it! After the infamous weakling Richard, who?'

'Henry,' Emmeline whispered.

'His number!'

'F . . . Fifth.'

The whole class was already rigid, and seemed to stiffen even more, as if not showing any emotion was their only safety. Except for their eyes, which all moved in fascinated horror, towards the dim object that hung behind the door.

Sarah sighed.

'Come down here!' Mrs Hubbard said.

Emmeline looked as if she would faint. 'Henry the Fourth,' she gasped. 'It was him I meant.'

'Indeed? I'm so glad to hear that, dearie. Don't keep me waiting.'

The girl came down. She was white; her hands clenched in front of her, her frizzy hair coming undone from the plait at the back. Her nose ran; she wiped it on her sleeve.

Mrs Hubbard turned majestically to Sarah. 'Fetch it,' she commanded.

Sarah frowned. She went slowly behind the desk to the dim corner. All eyes followed her.

The cane leaned in its darkness. This was its place; a thin sliver of power, barely seen, but it dominated the whole room, all their lives, their sleep. Not always the same one, of course; Mrs Hubbard wore out two or three a year. Now Sarah picked it up, seeing the ends of the bamboo were already split. It felt light and cruel, a swishing thing, ridged, the leather round the handle soiled with sweat, a hard grip. Every time she touched it she felt its attraction; she almost wanted to use it, to see how it would feel to wield that power.

Mrs Hubbard squeezed out of the pulpit, uncreasing and uncrackling like a great dark puffball of sweat and pomander oils, the black bun of her hair glossy and tight, stabbed with hairpins.

Emmeline sobbed. Something broke in her; all the pent-up agony came tumbling out. 'Please ma'am I'm sorry I'll learn it honest I will but don't give me the switch because me Da he gives me enough and he'll go mad he will . . .'

17

Mrs Hubbard smiled with pleasure. 'An enlightened parent. I'm sure you will learn it; I fully intend to present you, dearie, with a few reminders of your current failure. However, as it's such an important day, and I don't wish to get too . . . flustered, I will not use the cane.'

The class's silence was a blank astonishment.

Emmeline snivelled. 'You won't?' she sniffed, incredulous.

Mrs Hubbard took a large pinch of snuff. 'No, I won't.'

She inhaled the brown powder into her huge left nostril, then her right, and smiled.

'Sarah will do it instead.'

THREE

Somewhere outside, under the grey clouds, a gull began calling, a high, anxious mew.

Sarah felt its fear close round her. 'Me?' she said.

'You.' Mrs Hubbard's tiny black eyes watched her shrewdly. 'I've watched you, dearie. You're keen. You could have your own little place one day, just like this.' She glanced playfully at Emmeline. 'Five will do. Hand out, and if you flinch you'll have two extra.'

Sarah frowned, watching the little girl's palm rise up towards her, a small, trembling, fragile thing, pitifully dirty. Its openness beckoned her; part of her longed to crack down on it with the bamboo cane, to feel that quick swish end with the cry of pain. But the rest of her was annoyed. She didn't particularly care about Emmeline, or any of them. Sometimes she felt sorry for them. But it would be folly to lose her job over this. Five quick smacks and it would all be over.

Emmeline sobbed.

'Are you hesitating?' Mrs Hubbard snapped.

'Of course not.'

'Good. Don't forget you're just a menial here, girl. What are you?'

Sarah was silent.

Suddenly she saw the door at the back was open. There were footsteps, a rustle of silks. The visitors had finally arrived.

And with them stubbornness, that swept over her like a wave, so that she straightened her shoulders and drew up her chin. She was a Trevelyan, and all the pride clamped down inside her for so long came scorching up, a wave of heat in her neck and face. She glared at Mrs Hubbard's rolls of fat. And didn't answer.

The instant was huge as it passed; the terrible instant when Mrs Hubbard – and the class – realized the usual echo wouldn't be coming.

Mrs Hubbard's chest swelled with wrath. Appalled, the class watched. Emmeline's hand, wavering with weariness, descended and came abruptly up again.

Mrs Hubbard snatched the cane. 'I had high hopes of you. Thought you'd go far. But I know what this is, this is pride!'

She spat the word like venom. 'Always thought yourself a cut above the rest, haven't you dearie. A snobby little madam. Miss Sarah Trevelyan of Darkwater Hall, that's what you think you are. But your family were all drunks and tyrants and womanizers. And all I see is a scruffy little pupil-teacher on three shillings a week. Your face is red, your clothes stink, and there's a leak in one of your boots. That's the truth. That's all you are.'

And at the back of the room, suddenly, Sarah saw him watching her, the stranger from Darkwater Hall, the one they called Lord Azrael. Their eyes met; he looked sympathetic. She jerked her gaze away, silent with fury.

'Give the cuts,' Mrs Hubbard barked, 'or take them yourself.'

Sarah smiled, spiteful. 'I'll take them.'

Mrs Hubbard was sweating. Two threads of hair had unpinned from her glossy bun. She didn't know that behind her the doorway was dark with fascinated faces. Three ladies, four gentlemen, a faint breeze of perfume and cigar smoke heralding them like footmen. The class knew, without turning.

'You bare-faced, stinking, little . . .'

A masculine throat cleared, noisily. 'Is there a problem here, Ma'am, eh?'

Mrs Hubbard froze. Her face drained; only Sarah saw her struggle, the rigorous contortion of all hostility down to a single cold gleam in the eye. When she turned, she wore a sickly smile. For a moment Sarah almost admired her.

'Major Fleetwood! How wonderful to see you! Ladies! Please do come in.'

The red-whiskered man gave a beery laugh. 'Don't let us interrupt the necessary, ma'am. Discipline, eh! Know all about it. In India kept a fella just for whipping-in.' He strolled down between the tables and eyed Sarah blearily. 'This one blotted her copybook, eh?'

'This ungrateful wretch . . .' Mrs Hubbard took out her snuffbox, glanced at it, and thrust it back. '. . . was my pupil teacher. I have considered her conduct unsatisfactory for some time.'

'Bad show.' Major Fleetwood scratched his greasy hair. 'Trevelyan girl. Got anything to say?'

She had plenty. But she shook her head grimly.

Lord Azrael pushed forward. If he said anything, she thought, she'd die.

'Get on with it ma'am. No use prolonging the agony.'

'The ladies?' Mrs Hubbard whispered.

'Won't be too shocked. They have maids, Mrs H. And dogs.'

Sarah thrust her hand out, furious. It was even dirtier than Emmeline's.

'Look,' Lord Azrael said quietly. 'Whatever it was I'm sure she didn't mean it.'

'She's a fat bully,' Sarah said immediately. 'And I mean that.'

Mrs Hubbard went white. Then she brought the cane down, hard.

It whistled.

The pain was an explosion, a hot slash over the thick flesh of her thumb. Tears jerked into her eyes. She kept rigidly still.

Azrael looked shocked. She was glad.

Two. Three. Four.

Pain didn't repeat, it grew, swelling and throbbing into hugeness, spreading like a fire up her arm, neck, cheek. As the cane was raised for the last stroke she knew she would twitch, yell, scream, but she didn't; with a relentless fury she kept every inch of herself still, even when the molten, numbing flame stroked down. Only the slightest of indrawn hisses escaped her.

Five quick smacks, she told herself, scornfully.

'And that,' Mrs Hubbard gasped, slightly out of breath, 'hurts me as much as you. Such ingratitude, Major! I nurtured this girl. Gave her every opportunity. Even thought of her as my successor.'

'You can keep your situation.' Sarah put her sore hand under her arm. 'You were right about one thing. I do think myself above it. I'll make myself above it.'

She shoved past them, past Emmeline and the slightly unsteady Major, past the impressed and fugitive eyes of the class, straight through the cluster of ladies who crowded hurriedly back to make way. None of them looked at her. She was an embarrassment.

But as she passed him the stranger brought his gloved hand out of his pocket and said sadly, 'It would be a shame for you to go without your wages.'

His voice was low, with a curious friendliness.

'These are my wages,' she said hotly, opening her hand at him.

'I didn't mean that. Take this.'

He pressed it into her bruised fingers, then turned and limped between the desks. If it had been money she would have flung it after him, but it wasn't. It was a small rectangle of white card, quite empty on both sides.

She crumpled it in fury and stormed out, grabbing her shawl and running, out of the hateful stink of the place, down the lane, racing hard into the salt wind.

And then suddenly she was laughing, stupidly, leaping up on to walls and running along the tops, arms wide, chasing through the panicky sheep, jumping mud hollows and boulders, circling and giggling under the stunted thorn trees. The wind roared after her from the grey wilderness of the sea — it buffeted her and tossed her hair over her eyes and her cut hand was icy and numb but she didn't care.

She was free!

She had thrown it off like a smothering web, the filth, the endless, mindless bullying. And the books.

But for an exhilarated hour she didn't even care about those, racing till she was breathless along the cliff path and down the steep track into Newhaven Cove, all the gulls screaming and dizzying round her head.

She walked out on to the smooth sand. At first her

23

feet sank into the softness of it, leaving a trail of holes from the cliff, and then as it grew harder and more ridged she splashed through it, avoiding the coiled cast-heaps of worms and picking up tiny yellow shells. She threw one far out to sea, thinking, calmer now.

There had to be other jobs she could get. Down at the harbour, gutting fish. It was hard, but she could do it. Or at the china clay works. Then she remembered Major Fleetwood owned them. Not much chance there. Service then. A maid. She was quick. If someone gave her a chance, she'd learn. The thought of endless dirty dishes came to her; she squashed it, quickly.

It was past midday, but there was no point going home. After a while the sky darkened; it began to drizzle steadily, and the numbness in her hand wore off. It hurt now, throbbing hard, and she pulled it well into her sleeve out of the wind.

At the back of the cove the Darkwater came down the cliff in tiny falls; she turned and trudged back there, following her own solitary trail of prints over the empty, windswept sand.

For now, she thought, she wouldn't tell Martha, or her father. She'd find another job first. Whatever she did, though, on Saturday Martha would expect three shillings. Every week, money on the table. This week there'd be none. How would they eat? How would they manage? For a second, panic gripped her.

The Darkwater ran sluggishly into the sand. She crouched and washed her hot hand. Blood clouded the stream.

'Looks nasty, that.'

She turned, quick with surprise.

A tramp was huddled up under the overhang of the cliff, out of the wind. After a good look at him she turned back, plunging her swollen fingers into the stream. 'It is.'

'Strap?' he asked, interested.

'A cane.'

'Ah. Felt plenty of those meself, in me time.' His white hair was cut short, like stubble. She noticed he had quite a camp under the cliff, with a tin can boiling over a fire, and a scrawny dog gnawing something disgusting. The tramp edged up, against the rock.

'Made some space for thee.'

She stood, nervously. 'I have to get home.'

'Tha don't look eager. It's good soup. Warm you up.'

Sarah hesitated. The man looked old. His overcoat was tied with rope and the boots he wore had obviously been someone else's. He also had only one eye. The other was a blank emptiness; it fascinated her and she stared till she realised he was grinning.

'Sorry.'

'Used to it, girlie. Come on. I'm not dangerous.'

Clumsy in torn mittens he was pouring soup from the tin into a chipped mug and it smelled wonderful. She hadn't eaten since yesterday, so hungrily she sat opposite him and took it. Her right hand was swelling fast, red weals rising like the ridges in the sand.

'Cut and run?' he said, making a strange wheezing noise. She realized he was laughing.

'In a way.' Cautious, she tasted the liquid. It was hot, fishy. Salty. 'What's in this?'

He shrugged. 'Mussels. Samphire. Lobster.'

'Lobster!'

'Any fool can empty a creel.'

She drank it, gratefully, feeling its heat fill her. Taking the crust out of her pocket she dipped it in and chewed. Finally the tramp said, 'Did it meself, once.'

'What?'

'Cut and run.' He turned his empty eye on her. 'About thy age, I might have been. Lived in a fine great palace, very classy. Very high up. Landlord thought the world of me. The apple of his eye, I was.' He wheezed. 'Couldn't take to the work though. Started to think meself a bit above it. Had plans for meself.'

She took a thoughtful gulp. 'So what happened?'

A scatter of rain rattled from the gorse bushes. The tramp waved a mittened hand. 'Fell. Came down in the world. Took me a long time, to get this far.'

She stared, wondering. For a moment a sort of regret clouded him, then he wheezed out a laugh. 'Not that being gentry of the road don't bring its own rewards. Got something else to go to?'

'Not yet.' Emptying the mug she put it awkwardly on the sand; the dog knocked it over and licked the inside, avidly.

'Thanks for that. I'd better go now.'

'I know thee,' he said, slyly. 'Trevelyan's lass.'

She sighed. 'So?'

He winked. 'All them ancestors of thine. Tearing of their limbs and grinding their teeth while the devils pitchfork 'em. They ruled the folk round here for centuries, hard as nails. Now here's you, as low as low. How are we all fallen so far, eh?' He rubbed the dog's neck. 'But don't look back, that's what I say. Uses you up.'

As she stood he bent over and picked something up from the seaweed. 'Dropped something.'

It was the rectangular card. 'That's nothing,' she said, shortly.

'No? It's got letters on.' The tramp held it out. 'I know writing, though I'm no scholard.'

Surprised, she took it from his wet fingers.

It was the same card, but the words were vivid in neat pen strokes.

I FEEL I OWE YOUR FAMILY SOME RECOMPENSE. PLEASE COME AND SEE ME AT THE HALL. AZRAEL.

The tramp took out a bitten pipe and lit it. 'Good news?' he asked, slyly.

She stared at him in utter astonishment.

FOUR

That night she said to Martha, 'What's recompense?'

'Lord.' Martha took a pin out of her mouth and pushed it into the seam she was straightening. 'You're the book-learned one, Sarah. Some sort of debt. Paying back, like. Pence is money, isn't it?'

Sarah nodded. A hoarse call from the next room made her lift her head; she went to stand but Martha dumped the sewing in her lap.

'I'll go. Better for him not to see that, eh?'

As she went out Sarah flexed the bandaged hand gloomily. She'd take it off when she went in to see him. Otherwise he'd have one of his rages. She put Martha's sewing aside, got down on the sooty rag rug with its burned holes, and carefully put two more pieces of the precious sea-coal on the fire. For a moment she stayed there, in the meagre warmth, watching the yellow flames spurt.

At Darkwater Hall when she was small there must have been fires in every room, great roaring blazes. Sometimes she tried to remember it, but it was too long ago. There was a dream she had sometimes of a dining-room, sumptuous with chandeliers and cut-glass and candles, the tables heavy with food. Was that just imagination? Or had it been real?

After a while she took the white card out and read it again. COME AND SEE ME AT THE HALL.

Behind her the October gale rattled the bushes; they tapped on the window like fingers, as if the wet ghosts of the drowned had climbed the cliff path a few weeks early. She shivered, and crumpled the card. Then she dropped it into the fire and watched it curl. Blue flame burst from one corner. It crinkled into black tissue, and was gone.

The words had not been on it when he gave it to her. She was certain of that.

Martha came back and gathered up the sewing. She looked worried. 'I'm right glad the doctor's due tomorrow.' She glanced over the deft needle. 'We'll need to pay him, Sarah. There's only a half crown in the tin. Will Mrs Hubbard pay you this week?'

The anxiety was clear under her voice.

Sarah went cold. The panic she'd kept down all day bubbled up; she wanted to blurt it all out, that there wouldn't be any more money, that she'd thrown it all away in one stupid burst of anger. Instead she muttered, 'I expect so.'

To cover it, she got up and crossed to the window. Moving the nailed rag of curtain she let the wind gust into her face through the gaps in the frame. Reflected in the firelight she watched Martha sewing, a big, comfortable woman, pregnant again, almost slatternly, her long hair carelessly pinned.

'Can I ask you something?'

Martha looked up, surprised. 'If it's proper.'

'When I was a baby. When we lived in the Hall . . .'

Martha sighed. 'You know I can't talk about that. The master won't have it mentioned.'

'I just want to know!' Exasperated, Sarah turned.

'Nobody ever talks about it. I just want to know how it was! Did I have a big nursery? With a doll's house and rocking chair?'

Martha looked uncomfortable. She bit the thread.

'Were there chandeliers, like crystal, all down the stairs?'

'I can't talk of it. You know I can't.'

'And didn't you used to call me Miss Sarah?'

The shock made Martha stab her finger. With a hiss she sucked it, dropping the needle. When she looked up she was flushed.

'Of course I did. You were the master's daughter.'

'I still am.'

'Things have changed since then.' Martha took her handkerchief out and wrapped it tightly round her finger. Finally she said, 'Don't make your father's mistake, Sarah. Don't cling on to the old ways, thinking one day they'll come back. They won't. There's no house, no money. You're someone else now, as poor and downtrodden as the rest of us.'

'No!' Angrily Sarah turned her back. 'I'm still a Trevelyan. So is Papa. We don't belong here.'

Martha sucked the thread and pushed it through the needle's eye. 'The Trevelyans are finished,' she said firmly. 'And most people round here are only too glad.'

She tried everything. The old fishwives at the harbour laughed in her face, and the stinking piles of fishscales made her feel sick. At the factory with its smoking furnaces and dark gates she had to wait an hour before the foreman gave one look at her and said, 'No. Get lost.'

She went for service jobs in two houses; in both she

had to wait hours before being turned away.

The money was all gone. Her father's cough was worse. He asked for white bread, medicine, a tot of brandy, peevishly demanding how he was supposed to exist like this. By Thursday the stock of sea-coal was used up.

'We'll burn seaweed tomorrow,' Martha said grimly, brushing the dust up and sprinkling it on the fire.

The last, lowest humiliation was to go before the Poor Committee. She'd die first, she told herself, but she went, and then couldn't bring herself to go in, running away from the door, hot with shame.

There was nothing else to do and no one else to go to. And she was scared. So when Friday came, finally, bitterly, she wrapped the moth-eaten shawl around her shoulders and set off for Darkwater Hall.

The drive was over a mile long and deeply rutted. She trudged up it wearily, avoiding the puddles. Overhead the trees met in a tangle of stark bare twigs, and on each side the neglected undergrowth of yew and hazel and rowan grew so thick that in places it almost closed the track. The winter afternoon was bleak. In the bare elms jackdaws karked.

She was cold and uneasy. What sort of recompense was he thinking of? A job? She frowned. If he thought she'd be some skivvy in a house that should have been her own . . . Then she stumbled, and kicked the stone angrily. If he did, she had no choice.

The Hall rose up before her, its windows lightless. It was a huge building of some granite that was almost black, with awkward clusters of turrets and gables and under them a plainer, older facade. There were strange tales about the house. Not far off the river Darkwater disappeared underground; the country people said it ran under the very depths of the Hall, a roaring underground flood plunging down through some vast chasm into the depths of the earth. The river certainly went somewhere. Only a trickle ran on to the beach.

By the time she had crunched up the carriage sweep the sleet had begun to fall, faint and hissing. Behind her a glimmer of red lit the sky. She was soaked and hungry, hair plastered to her head; as she came under the front porch the gargoyles and monstrous griffins stared down, wide-eyed.

'Yes,' she snapped at them. 'The Trevelyans are back.'

She should go round to the servants' entrance, but she wouldn't. Half daring, half annoyed, she climbed the steps and pulled the bell.

It clanked.

Feeling small, she waited.

In the stained-glass windows the coat of arms of her family was dim in the gathering gloom. Falling leaves pattered on the stones. Beyond that the twilight was silent; so silent that a fox loped round the corner of the porch and peered at her with shrewd eyes. For a moment she wanted desperately to turn and run, down the drive, home, but there was nothing to run to but misery. Besides, it was too late.

Someone was unbolting the door.

The rattle made the fox slink into the bushes. Sarah turned, lifting her chin.

A small manservant opened the door. His shoulders were stooped, his hair lank and greasy. 'What?' he said, brusquely.

Sarah drew herself up. 'I'm here to see Lord Azrael. My name is Sarah Trevelyan.'

The man shrugged. ''Imself's choosy who 'e sees. Got an appointment 'ave you?'

'He asked me to come.' She wished she hadn't burned the card. It would have been good to flourish it in his face.

The man cocked his head slightly, as if listening to a voice she couldn't hear. Then he sighed and stepped back. 'Get yerself in.'

She walked up the steps into an octagonal hall. It was floored with black and white tiles, and she recognized the smell of it at once. It surged back at her from an immense distance, out of years of forgetfulness. Damp rooms, polish, cedarwood, the pressed petals of a hundred lost summers. As she breathed it in tears pricked her eyes, sudden and hot. She blinked them away in astonishment.

'Sit yerself down.' The servant indicated a chair with a grumpy wave. 'I'll see if 'is Lordship's 'ome.'

He crossed the hall, opened double doors and went through, closing them with both hands, giving her a shrewd, sardonic look. It reminded her of the fox.

Standing there, her skirt dripping into a pool, she knew for the first time just how far her family had fallen. Martha's cottage could fit twice into just this hall. The price of one of the paintings would feed the village for weeks. She looked up at their faces; men and women, stiff in gorgeous robes, gazing at her haughtily as if she was something far beneath them. The Trevelyans. Hard as nails.

She didn't sit. She would stain the striped yellow chair.

Even that seemed a precious thing, amazingly clean. There was a row of sculptures; she wandered along, looking at them. Roman. Or Greek. She wasn't sure. And how could one man live here on his own? With all his tenants crammed into squalid cottages like Martha's? It wasn't fair. It wasn't right. And yet she envied him.

The door to her right opened; the servant came through like a shadow.

'Aren't you the lucky one?' he said nastily. He scraped a match and lit a tall candle in a silver stick. 'Come up, 'e says. As if I 'aven't better things to do.'

He led her down a corridor to a great wooden staircase, its wide steps carpeted with softest wool. Her feet sank into luxury. Above were masses of clustering shapes that hung from the ceiling in the dimness, the vast chandeliers of her dreams. Draughts clinked their crystals; she felt their weight above her as she followed the small bent back, seeing the dandruff on his greasy collar.

The candle flickered along a landing, through a door and a lobby lined with blue and white vases to a wooden double door. The servant glanced at her and then knocked.

Someone murmured from inside.

The manservant opened the door. ' 'Ere she is. Beats me what you want with 'er.'

Surprised, Sarah stared at him. Then she straightened her soaked shawl and walked in.

Red light blinded her. It was streaming in through the high windows, a fiery glow like a vast furnace. For a second she almost felt it was burning her face, its heat roaring and crackling in the room. And then she saw

34

that the great salon faced west, and far out there over the sea the sun was setting, smouldering like a hot coal.

A fire burned in the grate. Sitting in a long chair by the window, his leg propped on a footstool and a black cat curled peacefully in his lap, was Lord Azrael. As he turned his head his dark face was lit by the flames.

'Sarah!' He stood, the cat jumping down with a mew of discontent. 'I'm so glad. I've been waiting for you to come.'

She stared at him. 'How did you know I would?'

'I knew, Sarah. I've known for years.'

'Years?' she whispered.

'Oh yes.' He smiled, a lopsided smile of shy pleasure. 'Years.'

FIVE

'Take that shawl, Scrab, and get it dried. And bring up tea, for both of us.' He turned to her, suddenly concerned. 'Did anyone come with you?'

'No,' she muttered. The man Scrab was taking the shawl from her shoulders in obvious disgust. She saw how frayed and dirty it was. Embarrassment burned her like the fireglow. What was she doing here?

'Sit here, please.' Azrael placed a chair near the fire and another for himself. He waited politely for her so she perched on its extreme edge, but the cushions were soft and forced her to lean back.

He sat too, the cat jumping up on to his knees. His long hands fondled its fur. There was a slight, awkward silence. The fire snapped noisily, the logs fizzing and spluttering.

She should be in the kitchens. Far below with some greasy cook yelling at her. Perhaps the doubt showed in her face, because he smiled; a dark, sideways smile. She felt annoyed.

'What did you mean, you've expected me for years?' she asked hotly.

Lord Azrael rubbed the cat's back. It arched, purring. Instead of answering he said quietly, 'You must hate me.'

It startled her. She wanted to say yes, but it wouldn't have been true. 'I want to.'

'But you don't?'

'I don't know you.'

'But I have your estate. All of it. You must feel bitter; the way you have to live now . . .'

'All right.' She shrugged. 'But it's my grandfather, if it's anyone. I don't understand how he could be so stupid! Nobody's ever explained to me how it happened. About your father and him.'

Azrael smoothed the cat's ears. Then he glanced at her, his dark clipped beard catching the fireglints. 'It wasn't my father that won the house. It was me.'

She stared, amazed. 'You! But it was fifteen years ago. You don't look . . .' Confused, she stopped.

'Old enough? Thank you, Sarah. But it was me. Has no one really ever told you?'

'I'm not allowed to ask. It drives Papa into one of his fits.'

'Then I'll tell you. I think that's only fair.' He pushed the cat down. It sat on the tasselled hearthrug and began to lick itself.

Azrael put the tips of his fingers together. 'You never really knew your grandfather. Such a proud man. Old Squire Trevelyan they called him, and he could recite every one of his ancestors back to Doomsday. Often did, when he was drunk. A loud, roaring, boasting, relentless man. If his tenants couldn't pay he turned them out. He had no mercy. He once shot a man who'd caught a rabbit on his land. Eight children, and one rabbit to feed them. Shot him dead, Sarah. It's said the young widow stood up in church and prayed the devil would come for his soul. Like all your family – forgive me – he was heartily despised.'

It wasn't such a shock. She'd guessed most of it.

Azrael stared into the flames. 'One night, it happened that we were both among a shooting party of gentlemen, and the weather drove us indoors, to an inn called the Black Dog, far out on Bodmin Moor. He had drunk too much. All night we played cards. The others in the group gradually dropped out of the game, until only we two were left. I was winning; my luck was good that night, and I was young and thought it was a fine thing. Finally, the Squire ran out of money. I told him the game was over.

'What a rage he flew into! Swearing and throwing over tables and threatening all of us with death and hell until the innkeeper begged me to play on. I wasn't averse. I thought he deserved a lesson.

'First, he bet his horse, and lost it. Then all his horses. Then a farm, his hounds, his fishing rights, his mine. He was desperate by then, face red and contorted with fury. I stood up, but he grabbed my arm and drew a pistol, cocking it and pointing it at my head. For a while I thought he'd murder me on the spot; his cronies were all round him and we were far out on the moor. "This time," he snarled "we bet everything. Winner takes all. Everything we own, estate, house, life, soul. On the turn of a card." '

He glanced at her. 'You think I should have refused.'

'Of course I do!'

'Yes. But remember, the gamble was the same for both of us. Either could have lost everything – I had large estates myself. I was intrigued, and really too scared to refuse. And . . .' Azrael shrugged ruefully. 'I was sorry for him. Ruin was staring him in the face. He wanted one more chance. So, I agreed.'

For a moment there was silence in the room, the only sound the tiny rasp of the cat's tongue on its fur.

Then Azrael said, 'The innkeeper brought a clean deck of cards. He shuffled them. Your grandfather was to draw first. All around us the drinkers and packmen and poachers crowded close, the air stifling with cheap tobacco and the fumes of smuggled brandy. His hand shook; he swore a terrible oath, and cut the pack. "Let the devil take me and all mine to hell," he yelled "if I fail in this." Then he turned the card. It was the King of Diamonds.

'Of course, he thought he had won. The crowd roared, clapping and whistling. He pushed the pack towards me, with such a triumph on his face, and by God, Sarah, if I could have turned tail and fled at that moment I would have done it. But a wager is a wager. I reached out, and turned a card.'

'What did you get?' she whispered, knowing already.

Firelight flickered on his face. Quietly he said, 'The Ace of Spades.'

With a creak that made her jump, the door opened. Scrab backed in with a large tray, laid it down on the table and put a kettle on a small stand near the fire. He was muttering peevishly.

'What's the matter?' Azrael asked.

'Naught you'd care for,' the man said sourly.

Azrael smiled at Sarah. 'Really,' he whispered, 'he's got a heart of gold.'

Scrab spat into the fire, and arranged the teacups, noisily. They were porcelain, Sarah noticed, incredibly fragile. Azrael sat back, watching; quickly she glanced around the dim room, seeing its marble tables, sculptures, the piano on its dais. The warm glow of the sunset had waned; now Scrab touched a taper to the fire and went round lighting candles, tall white expensive candles in silver holders. Sarah thought of Martha's scrapings of rushlights and frowned. Heavy red curtains swished shut across the windows, closing out the wet evening. The room was perfect. It enclosed her in warmth and security, like a womb.

'That will do, Scrab,' Azrael said lazily.

When the man had scuttled out she said, 'What happened to my grandfather?'

Uneasy, Azrael leaned over and poured tea from the china teapot. 'He was found, two days later, at the foot of the cliffs at Newhaven. He may have fallen over in the dark. Or perhaps, the shame . . .'

Sarah stood up so abruptly that the cat turned, eyes wide.

'That was your fault.' Suddenly she was so angry it trembled through her. 'You should have told him you didn't want the wretched estate!'

'I did.' Azrael was calm. 'I swore before all of them I wouldn't take it. I didn't want his ruin. But he was proud. No Trevelyan, he roared, would ever go back on his word. If he had to start again without a penny, he would! He had courage, Sarah. Just like you. If it had been you, you'd have been too proud to ask for your losses back. You'd rather have died.'

Slowly, she sat. He handed her a cup and she took it, reluctant.

'Try the cakes. The cook is really very good at them.'

They would have choked her, she thought. 'No thanks. So you got everything.'

'Everything. House, estate, paintings, horses, even the sheets on the beds and the flowers wilting in the vases. I won his past from him and your future from you. That's why I want to help you now.'

She took a swallow of the hot tea. It made her feel better. 'How?'

40

He lifted a small iced cake daintily with silver tongs. 'You've lost your situation.'

'Because I was stupid.'

'Is that why?'

'She wanted me to beat Emmeline,' Sarah said coldly, 'and I wouldn't. The poor little wretch has enough troubles. I felt sorry for her.'

He was silent a moment, patting his knee till the cat jumped up. When he spoke again his voice was almost sly. 'It didn't seem like that to me.'

She stared.

'No, to me it seemed you were quite ready to cane the child. You didn't care for it, but you would have done it. No, the reason you rebelled was that the woman Hubbard called you a menial, in front of me, and told you to repeat it. That stuck in your throat.' He smiled. 'Just like a Trevelyan.'

Sarah put the cup down, so hard that it clinked in the saucer and toppled over. 'Why have you brought me here? Just to make fun of me?'

'Indeed no. To offer you a new situation.'

She stood, furious. 'As some scullerymaid.'

Azrael's eyes widened. He swung his legs off the footstool and swivelled round, concerned. 'Of course not! Was that what you thought?'

'I don't know what to think!'

'Please, sit down.'

But she didn't move so he took a breath and said, 'I'm a reclusive man, Sarah. Something of a scholar; my field is alchemy and all the strange old sciences of the Middle Ages. Old-fashioned now, of course, with our gas lamps and steam engines. But important to me. The Great Work, the old sages called it.' He leaned forward, his face keen and lit with enthusiasm. 'The eternal, unending search for the most precious element in the universe. For pure gold, Sarah! For shining goodness!'

As if he'd said too much he stopped, and laughed. 'I have a laboratory and an immense library, thousands of volumes, all untidy and muddled, that desperately need to be put in order and catalogued. I also need help with my experiments. I would like to pay you to do it. Twelve shillings a week, and all found. Rooms for yourself and your father, here in the Hall. He will be well looked after.'

She stared down at him, utterly astonished.

He smiled, picked the cat up again, and smudged crumbs off the cake. The cat's pink tongue licked them from his finger. 'Do please accept. I have no desire for fussy secretaries or prying university men. I want someone who loves learning. And don't just think I've invented this for your sake. Believe me, I really need the assistance. You've seen Scrab.'

She sank back into the chair, legs suddenly weak. 'How do you know I like learning?'

His glance was bright and amused. 'Why else would you stay at that bearpit of a school? No, you'd be perfect, Sarah. We could work well together on my Great Work, to make gold, the most precious of things. Do say yes. But take time to think, if you want.'

The fire crackled. Around her the portraits of cruel Trevelyans stared down at her scornfully. She knew she was betraying them by taking a job in their house. In her house. But back at the cottage her father would be coughing.

'I accept,' she said.

SIX

Martha picked up the pile of shining coins and clicked them through her fingers. Then she dropped them back on the scrubbed boards of the table. 'It's a lot extra,' she said.

'Mmm,' Sarah blew on the spoonful of potato soup and swallowed it even though it burned her tongue. She wondered how to explain.

In the weak rushlight the page next to her chipped plate was shadowy. It was a battered dictionary, one of her father's few possessions. She tore a chunk off the loaf, reading.

ALCHEMY *The medieval science of the Philosopher's Stone, the search to transmute metals into gold.*

Instantly, like a blow out of nowhere, the memory of her strange dream came back. She stopped eating, spoon paused in mid-air. The Library. It was coming true.

She was so amazed she almost didn't notice Martha had sat down opposite. Martha never sat down in the mornings. There was too much to do.

The stout woman pushed back her greying hair. Then she said, 'Or did His Lordship give you the money?'

Alarmed, Sarah stared. 'What?'

Martha sighed. 'Lord, Sarah, don't play miss innocent. I know Mrs Hubbard turned you away. I heard about it at the market yesterday.'

Sarah dropped the spoon into the dish. 'She didn't turn me away. I left.'

'It's all the same in the end.'

The baby gurgled in its crib; she gave it an anxious glance. 'You've got your rent,' Sarah said hotly.

'Yes, but I'm worried about you. Lord Azrael . . .'

'What on earth makes you think I got it from him?'

'This.' Quickly, as if she didn't like to touch it, Martha took a small white card from her pinafore and laid it on the table.

Sarah stared at it with cold fear. She had burned this. She'd watched it turn black and crinkle and fall into ash.

She reached out and turned it over; it felt smooth and cool. The familiar words slid over its surface.

I FEEL I OWE YOUR FAMILY SOME RECOMPENSE.

For a second there was something darkly mocking in the sloping script.

'It was in the ashes when I cleaned the grate.' Martha leaned forward and caught hold of Sarah's wrist. 'What does it mean? Why does he want to make all right, after years and years?'

'It's nothing. He's given me a situation. In his Library.'

'His Library?' Martha looked puzzled. 'With books? But why you? There's learned folk would suit him better . . .'

Annoyed, Sarah pulled away. She took the soup dish to the scullery and scrubbed it fiercely in the cold greasy water. 'Well, he's asked me. He's paying twelve shillings all found.'

'You're to live in!'

Exasperated, Sarah turned. 'All servants live in, Martha, and that's all I'll be. There's a room for Papa too. It'll be better for him than here. More like he's used to.'

Even as she said it she saw Martha's shock.

'But who'll take care of him, the master? I always have! He knows me.'

'There'll be servants.'

'Yes, and how they'll despise him!'

'I thought you'd be pleased,' Sarah snapped. 'Or is it the rent you'll really be missing?'

In the silence she knew it had been a spiteful thing to say. Martha turned and bent over the cradle; after a second Sarah crossed to the back door and opened it, feeling the wet breeze on her face, the wild cries of gulls over the ploughed fields on Marazy Head. Out at sea a faint drizzle obscured the fishing fleet.

After a long breath she said, 'Sorry.'

Martha had the baby out and was rocking it. Her face was flushed. 'There's talk about this Azrael,' she said, obstinately. 'That he spends nights in sorcery and speaking with demons. No one respectable goes near the Hall after dark. They say he's found a way down to the caverns, and sometimes at night you can hear a roar like great engines churning underground. Ernie Marsden that lives out on the cliff says on full moon last week he looked out and saw the carriage there, and His Lordship walking, at dead of night, looking over the sea. He's a strange man, that's for sure.'

Sarah shrugged. 'Gossip. He's a scholar. And a gentleman.'

'Indeed? They say the devil is a gentleman.'

The dry voice came from the bedroom. Sarah jerked round in alarm.

Her father stood there, supporting himself on his silver-topped cane. His face was mottled, and the black and gold silk dressing-gown that had once been expensive fell loose round his thin body. He breathed heavily.

'You shouldn't be up!' Martha hissed. She gave the baby to Sarah and brought a chair quickly to the fire. Then she tried to take his arm.

'Don't fuss me, woman!' He lowered himself stiffly, chest heaving. It took him a painful minute to catch his breath; then he glared at Sarah. 'So. You seriously expect me to go back to Darkwater Hall.'

'I thought . . .'

'You didn't think!' His hands shook on the stained silver knob. 'Not if you imagined that I would even cross the threshold with that . . . upstart living there. See my daughter a skivvy in her own house! Stay cooped in some attic and watch him . . . sitting in my chairs . . . eating from my table . . . taking the very food from our mouths!' His breath rattled; he spat into the fire. 'What sort of Trevelyan have I bred? I'd starve here first.'

Azrael had been right, she thought grimly. This whole mess had come from pride, and it was still crippling their lives. Well, she'd be the one to end it.

'I'm going,' she said, firmly but quietly. 'We need the money and he wants to make amends. If you don't approve Papa, then stay here. We can afford the rent.'

Martha had taken the baby into the tiny scullery. They heard him wail in dismay as he was washed.

Her father looked at her. He was so shrunken, every

breath an effort. The silver cane and silk gown she had known all her life looked pathetic now, soiled bits of the past that he clung to obstinately. His weakness frightened her. She came and crouched by the chair.

'Don't forbid me. Because I'd have to go anyway. I know it's hard. But would you rather me be some fishwife, stinking of herring, or go cap in hand to the workhouse? At least this is a job, something respectable.'

She waited, but he didn't answer.

They both knew she had to go, but he would never admit to it.

She stood up, wearily. 'I'll get my things together. I'll be home on my day off.'

It wasn't until she reached the truckle bed that he put his head in his hands.

'How in God's name did we sink to this?' he muttered.

There was little to pack — a few clothes, her mother's cameo brooch, an old notebook, all stuffed into one of Jack's sacks. He had come in from the fishing and was watching, uneasy. 'Any trouble, Sarah,' he muttered 'and you come back. Just come back.'

'Thanks, Jack,' she said, tying the sack up. Her father had gone back to his room. She glanced at the closed curtain. 'Look after him, won't you?'

'Don't you worry. We will.'

Outside, she walked to the stile, climbed it and looked back at the cottage. On the doorstep, Martha was waving the baby's tiny fist.

In the deep lane the wind died away. Between the stone walls a flock of bramblings scattered into the bare thorns of gorse. She walked quickly. There was no point looking back. And there was something inside her, she knew, that was glad, that wanted those warm, comfortable rooms, the soft carpets, the sense of being someone.

She took the short cut over the fields and into Darkwater woods. Usually she would have avoided this track, but she felt reckless and free and it was quicker than walking up the drive. Most of the Darkwater estate was farmland, with small wooded ravines and coombs in the folds of the cliffs. Every bay and cove along this coast belonged to it, every shipwreck, all the rents of the tenantry in the tiny hamlets, Cooper's Cross, Durrow, Mamble, even the tollgate on the road to Truro. And these woods around Darkwater Hall, an ancient wildwood hardly thinned or managed, threaded with mysterious paths.

She knew the way. But the drizzle thickened; a grey soaking mist moving in from the sea as the short afternoon waned. It hung round her like a fog. She stopped, one hand on a damp oak trunk, listening.

The wood was silent. No birds. No gulls. Only the sea-mist, closing quietly.

For a moment doubt about the whole thing overtook her. She weighed the sack, uneasy. Maybe she should go back. Maybe Martha was right. Then, just ahead, in the greyness, something loomed, and she groped towards it through the brambles and felt its cold hollows with her fingers.

Stone.

It was one of the Quoits.

She jerked her fingers back, instantly. The Devil's Quoits, everyone called them. The story was that the devil had thrown them from the cliffs, aiming at the tower of the church, but they'd fallen here, a line of three leaning stones. That was another superstition. It might suit Jack and Martha, but not her. In one of the books in the school she'd read that stones like these were put up by people thousands of years ago. Still, she didn't like them.

They leaned in the fog. Faint lichen grew on them, green splotches of spores, and they were scored with long grooves, as if by great claws. They barred her way. She'd go home.

Instantly, not far behind, a dog growled.

The sound made her flesh crawl. She turned and looked back.

A padding of paws rustled and pattered in the thick drifts of invisible leaves. And then, far back in the smothers of drizzle, a great black shape was running towards her, muscled and lean, tongue lolling out, eyes like tiny red coals.

She turned and fled. Breathless and gasping she struggled frantically through branches that whipped into her face, thickets of conifer and holly. All the fog seemed to be panting at her heels; behind her it thudded as if a pack of spectral hounds, dark as mist, was hunting her down, running with her, and as she ducked under a yew into darkness she stifled a scream, feeling a hot wet tongue on her neck, teeth catching her shawl. The fabric tore; yelling, she struck out at nothing with the sack, stumbling back out of branches into sudden space, a clipped hedge, a gravel walk.

At once she turned and raced along it, under the dark fog-wreathed mass of the house towards the slot of light that was opening. Yellow lamp light streamed out; it sent her shadow out behind her, stretched and flitting, and she had a sudden horror that the shadow-hound would grab it and gnaw it, but even as she turned to look the door was pulled wide and the terrace walk above the sunken garden was empty but for drifts of fog through the light.

'For Gawd's sake,' a voice said irritably. 'I'm not standing 'ere all night!'

Scrab held the lantern up, eying her bedraggled breathless panic. Between his feet the cat slithered in, its fur soaked.

She slid in and slammed the door. It felt solid at her back.

Scrab turned. For a moment she thought he was grinning. 'Welcome 'ome,' was all he said.

SEVEN

The dress was dark blue, with an ivory lace collar. It lay spread on the bed and she stared at it in silent wonder.

Scrab dumped the candle on the fireside table. ' 'Imself says you might not want to get yer breakfast with the workers. So . . .'

'Yes.' She nodded, decisively. 'I will.'

He shrugged, scattering dandruff. 'Please yerself. 'Servants' 'All. Seven. Now can a man get to 'is bed?'

She summoned as much dignity as she could, 'Yes. Thank you.'

When he had closed the door she dumped the sack on the floor and collapsed on to the bed's edge, running both hands through her soaked hair. What a way to come home! Because it was home. Or should have been.

The thought gave her a sort of courage. Smelling toast, she raised her head and saw on a tiny round table by the fire a tray laid with the same porcelain cup and teapot that she had seen downstairs. Unlacing her boots she kicked them off, washed face and hands in the basin on the washstand, pulled her old nightdress on and curled luxuriously in the velvet chair, enjoying the small clear flames and eating the toast slowly, its warm golden butter dripping on to her fingers.

This was bliss. And Scrab hadn't brought it; it had been here waiting. Azrael had been that sure she would come.

Wriggling her toes in the heat she thought for a

moment of her father, coughing in his bed in the draughty cottage, but she poured the tea out quickly and tried to forget. The money would make things better for him. But if only he would have come!

She looked round. The bedroom was small, but not a garret, its walls papered a deep red. The bed lay under a heavy coverlet, and in dimmer corners dark furniture lurked. A press, a tallboy, a small closet by the wall. The windows were shuttered. Tomorrow, she thought sleepily, she would look at it all, but she was far too tired now. But she did cross the soft carpet and open the closet, warily.

A tiny moth flitted from its cedar-scented darkness. It was empty, except for a big dark book, which she lifted down. It was a Bible. There was a clasp on it, but it wasn't locked, and a long white feather had been pushed into one of the pages. It was heavy, and she took it to the bed.

The feather puzzled her. It was far too long for any bird she knew. It glistened, and there was a faint sweet smell on it. Sleepily, she gazed at the page it had marked.

'Thy pomp is brought down to the grave, and the noise of thy viols; the worm is spread under thee, and the worms cover thee.

How art thou fallen from heaven, O Lucifer, son of the morning.'

It was the story of the proud angel that had been cast out from heaven in the great war of the powers of light and darkness; Lucifer, who had become devious and evil, become Satan. Not the sort of thing to read at night.

The candle spluttered. She put the Bible on the table,

climbed under the heavy quilt, and blew out the flame.

Something the tramp had said whispered through her head.

'*How are we all fallen so far?*'

Only once did she waken.

Very late, it must have been. The moon had risen; as she opened her eyes she saw how it silvered the thinnest edge of the looking-glass. Sarah lay stiff. The fire had sunk to a glow. All around her in its black stillness, Darkwater Hall lay sleeping.

Except for the footsteps.

Faint in the darkness, they creaked the boards on the narrow stair outside her room. Hardly breathing, sweat prickling her back, she raised her head and listened for them. Down the corridor they came, over the canvas matting; a slow step, halting.

She turned over, soundlessly, staring through the dark in terror at her door, at the faint slot of glimmering light under it, but the footsteps went straight past, even and steady, like a man sleepwalking or lost in thought.

She didn't light the candle.

Instead she swung her legs out, unlocked the door and opened it, a tiny fraction. Cold draughts stirred her hair. She put her eye to the crack.

The corridor was dim. Small moonlit squares slanted across it. At the far end was a door and she saw that someone was there, unlocking it. Keys clinked.

It might have been Azrael; in the dimness she couldn't tell, except that whoever it was was tall, and wore some dark robe. He opened the door.

And she heard, just for a moment, the distant,

unmistakeable sound of water; deep, running water, echoing in vast underground hollows.

Then he was gone.

Bolts were slotted tight.

The house was still.

Breakfast would be an ordeal, if they were all like Scrab. She put the blue dress on, tidied her hair and looked at herself thoughtfully in the mirror. 'Don't say much. Be dignified. Listen. Find out how things run.'

First, though, she went to look at the door at the end of the corridor, but when she got there she found only a long tapestry with some dusty hunting scenes on. She lifted it and groped behind but the wall was solid and pannelled and thick with dust.

Bewildered, she let the folds drop, rubbing her hands. Had she dreamed it? She didn't think so.

Uneasy, she found her way down. It had been dark last night, with only Scrab's candle flickering in the shadows, and this morning in the cold sunlight the house seemed very different. At the bottom of the stairs passages ran both ways, flagstoned and silent. She paused, hoping someone might come along.

It was very quiet. There was none of the bustle she had expected. Instead she had the strangest feeling that she was alone in this place, the only mortal here. And she didn't quite feel the same. The wet scared girl who had arrived last night seemed like someone different, as if this new Sarah in the blue dress, the finest dress she had ever worn, was a lost being who had come home.

She found another staircase and swished down it. Everything was clean. There was no dust, no cobwebs.

There had to be an army of servants in a vast place like this.

But the Servants' Hall, when she found it, was quiet. A few plates lay on the tables, as if people had come and gone, but in the vast kitchens only a red-faced cook and a boot-boy were peeling potatoes.

'Help yourself, miss,' the woman said cheerily.

Sarah did, puzzled. Where were the housemaids and grooms, the scullery maids, valet, butler and footmen? Where were the gardeners and coachmen, the skivvies and parlourmaids? Surely they must be here.

She lifted a salver off a dish and found porridge. Another covered something made of scrambled eggs and rolled spicy pieces of mackerel. She ate porridge first, then piled some of the other on her plate, feeling the heavy knife and fork with satisfaction. In the kitchen the cook gossiped to the boy. Neither took any notice of her.

Just as she was feeling uncomfortably full the cat came in. It sat on the mat in front of the great range and began to wash its tail. She watched it, thinking of the black hound in the wood.

'Lord Azrael's compliments,' Scrab said hoarsely, making her jump, 'and if yer ready I'm to fetch you to the Library.'

She brushed off crumbs. 'I'm ready.'

As she went out, the cat paused in its licking. It gave her one small, watchful glance.

On the way she asked Scrab about the servants. He scowled, sucking his teeth. ' 'Imself's a recluse. Likes a quiet 'ouse. The cook and I look after 'im.'

'No one else?'

'Boy, for odd jobs. Coachman. If 'e wants anyone else 'e gets 'em from the other place.'

She was silent a moment, lifting the hem of her dress as they climbed the great stair. 'He's very rich then?'

'Rich enough.'

'These other estates. Where are they?'

Ahead of her, Scrab flicked a sour glance over one stooped shoulder. 'Never you mind,' he muttered.

His breath stank of onions.

The door closed behind her; she heard him walk away.

Slowly she shook her head in bewilderment.

This was the landscape of her dream. A corridor, very narrow, and all down it, as far into the distance as the light allowed, she saw books, great shelves of them, floor to ceiling; nightmarish numbers of books, chained, leatherbound, clasped, hinged. She walked under them, feeling their awe. On each side were doors; peering through she found a series of small rooms, linking with each other, as if this whole wing was a maze of learning, and in them all more books, a muddled confusion of stacks and opened volumes. On the walls stuffed animals gazed down at her glassily; between the two windows of the third room a double-horned rhino mouldered, with the plaque SHOT IN THE AFRICAN WILDERNESS BY JOHN WILLIAM TREVELYAN 1842 proudly emblazoned under it.

Outside, the winter lawns were bleak. Gulls squealed over the grey sea.

She wandered the rooms, picking things up, turning pages, wondering hungrily how and where she would start. This would take years to sort out. It pleased her, gave her a sudden, secret satisfaction.

The last room was the Laboratory.

She opened the door and peered in, then knocked, nervously, but no one was here. It was dim; all the window shutters firmly closed. She crossed to one and lifted the bar. The shutter swung inward; daylight turned the room cold.

She saw strange balls of glass that hung from the gilt ceiling, slowly rotating. All the walls were painted with huge, brilliant frescoes; blue and gold and green, great Zodiac figures, the Goat, the Fish, the Scorpion, and over the fireplace strange symbols of sun and moon and stars. Even the small coloured tiles in the hearth had odd foreign letters and twisted snakes. Machines, scales, peculiar devices littered every surface.

On the benches she walked between were open books, some centuries old, and scattered about them in total confusion strange objects; tubes of evil-smelling stuff, saucers of acrid powder, glass retorts with liquids plopping and boiling inside. She picked up a mothy furred thing and dropped it with a hiss of horror; it was the mummified paw of a small monkey, and she rubbed her hand hurriedly on her dress.

The room smelt musty and sulphureous. Astrolabes and globes and other instruments she didn't even recognize were piled around. An Egyptian figure with a jackal's head held down a stack of papers; lifting the top sheet she found it was covered with the dark sloping writing that had been on her card. There were notebooks of scribble and diagrams; carefully drawn wheels, a man with all the muscles outlined in his body, arrowed with unreadable symbols she guessed might be Greek.

Then, in the far corner, something shifted.

She dropped the papers and stared over. There was a clutter of things there, an hourglass with sand running through and a lamp, but the movement had been behind those. Curious, she pushed through the benches and came closer.

She saw a tall glass dome. Somehow it seemed faintly lit from inside, as if lined with some phosphorescent material. Above it was a card with the word GEMINI scrawled on, and a drawing of twin embryos linked together, so realistic it made her feel sick.

As she lifted her hand, something moved inside the dome.

She stopped. Had it been her reflection?

And then she saw that a boy was sitting in the dome; tiny and far away, but alive. Real! He was reading, his hair short and oddly-cut, his clothes strange. He looked well-fed and healthy. She recognized him; he was the boy in her dream, so she crouched, fascinated, her huge face level with him.

How had Azrael imprisoned him here? Tales of horrors crept into her mind, of created beings, things grown from parts of dead men.

'Can you hear me?' she breathed.

The boy ignored her. He pushed a small white box into the wall where it stuck, and made a click. A lamp lit next to him by magic. And she saw she was wrong; it wasn't one boy but two, one dissolving out of the other, identical, and the second twin could see her, because he jumped up and pointed and his brother turned and said, 'Where?'

Sarah leapt back. Her skirt caught the dome. It

wobbled and she grabbed it in terror, the two boys tumbling about inside like toys, and the door opened behind her and in the mirror she saw Azrael's face, white with shock.

'For God's sake!' he hissed. 'Don't drop that!'

EIGHT

Azrael drew a black curtain around the dome and pushed it into a small wall-safe, which he locked with a key on his watch-chain. Then he came over and leaned against the bench, arms folded. His face was grave, and still pale. She couldn't tell how angry he was. She clasped her hands behind her back, stopping herself from bursting out with ridiculous excuses.

'Well,' he said finally. 'Perhaps Mother Hubbard was right. You are a trouble-maker, after all.'

'Changed your mind?' she murmured.

He smiled. 'Once I set my sights on someone, Sarah, I never change my mind. But there ought to be some rules, don't you think? The first can be that you never enter this particular room without me.' He picked up a smooth egg-shaped stone and rubbed it with acid-scarred fingers, as if self-conscious. She almost felt disappointed. So she said 'What was in that thing?'

He looked up, sly. 'What do you think?'

'I saw . . . two boys. Twins. They were real, like live people. How can you keep them in there? Won't they suffocate?'

He smiled, shaking his head. 'Oh, Sarah. Your education has been neglected. How we'll change all that.' He put the stone down and limped down the bench, putting things back in their places. Then he took his topcoat off, tied a white apron on, and began to stir and examine the retorts. 'What you saw was best described as an image. Real, but not real.'

'I saw it,' she said, stubborn.

'A vision. Beings that might exist elsewhere.'

'Spirits?'

'In a manner of speaking.'

The cat had come in. It picked its way along the bench delicately, over shells and carved wood and models of insects. Then it looked at her and mewed.

'Yes,' Azrael said absently. 'Quite right. Mephisto says it's time you started work.'

She stared at him. 'Sorting the books?'

'Indeed.'

'Where do I start?'

He shrugged. 'Wherever you wish. You'll find everything you need out in the Rhino room. Take your time. Enjoy yourself.' He stroked his dark faint beard and lifted an eyebrow. 'After all, this isn't Mrs Hubbard's academy. This is another world, Sarah.'

And it was. It was heaven. She could hardly believe she had fallen into it. There were books of history, Greek plays and Roman battles, atlases and prints of beautiful paintings; there were poems and novels and scattered pages of strange music and hundreds of sepia photographs of Egyptian mummy cases, their painted eyes wide. Above all there were the mysterious and magical books of alchemy, bound in calf and leather, their stiff pages closely covered with the dark letters of unknown languages, of spells and philosophic musings and recipes and diagrams.

The quest for gold fascinated her. What process could

transmute dull metal into a shining beauty? What sort of power would that be?

For hours she just browsed and read, turning strange, wonderful pages. Scrab shuffled up with a tray at some time but she barely noticed him; later, when she realised she was hungry, the food had long gone cold, the afternoon dark. She hadn't eaten a thing, caught up in the enchantment and glory of the books.

Her head felt muzzy, her eyes tired. Picking up some meat and stiffened bread she chewed it in delight, then crossed to the casement and opened it, letting a cold sea-wind straight in.

Far out over the fishing fleet the gulls and terns made screeching clouds; the lobsterpots were being lifted. Below, Lord Azrael was coming up the track on a pale horse. She hadn't even heard him go out. Scrab came down to meet him, greasy coat gleaming.

Azrael waved up at her. 'Don't strain your eyes,' he laughed, the wind flapping his collar.

She shrugged. 'I haven't even started yet,' she whispered to herself.

It was easy to forget, in the Library. All week she lived in its warm cocoon. The books were a spell; once she touched them their stories and knowledge held her tight. Gradually she worked out a careful plan; to get them all down, room by room, shelf by shelf, and sort them into categories – history, science, religion – and then to number them, making accurate lists. There were thousands, and it would take years to do, even if she could stop herself reading them, but the idea exhilarated her. Already she had discovered a whole cupboard full of chained Bibles in unknown alphabets; the unknowable squiggles of their letters fascinating her. She had to force herself to get out and get some air, walking between the heavy October showers to the beach where the hard sand was pitted with rain marks. She ate her meals alone and she slept deeply, as if all the worries of the world had been wiped away. Twice, sleepily, she thought she heard the distant unbolting of a door, and sometimes through her dreams ran the deep thunder of a hidden river, far below her pillow, echoing in the foundations and walls and vast chimneys of the old house.

And she didn't go home. She didn't even think of the cottage until Azrael mentioned it. Late on the night before Hallowe'en, she helped him open the great casements in the Laboratory and wheel out the brass telescope. Scrab was there too, muttering in disgust at the oil on his hands.

'What you want with this contraption,' he said sourly, 'I don't know.' He ran a dark eye round the room. 'Nor yet the rest of the junk I 'ave to clean.'

Azrael smiled. 'All knowledge is in the heavens, Scrab.'

'And in 'Ell, more like.' He shuffled out, wiping his palms on his sleeves.

'Why do you put up with him?' Sarah asked.

Azrael looked surprised. 'He's an old family retainer. I'd miss him, if he went. He's devoted to me, of course.'

'It doesn't look like it.'

He smiled, sitting at the eyepiece, and turned the scope to face the moon, adjusting the focus carefully. 'And as for you, well, tomorrow is Sunday. Your day off. You must go to church, and then home.'

'There's too much to read,' she said, evasively.

'It will wait. You'll have a lifetime to read it all. Maybe more.'

She stared at him but he was taking notes in the moonlight. So she said, 'What if I don't want to go?'

'You must. Otherwise my name will be further blackened in parish gossip. Sarah Trevelyan kidnapped and held against her will!'

He swivelled round, his face lit with mischief. 'Or they'll say we play cards eternally for the soul of your grandfather!'

The idea seemed to amuse him. He got up, took a pack from a drawer and slapped them down in front of her. 'Shall we, Sarah?'

'Don't make a joke of it.'

'I'm not! I mean it. Cut the pack.'

Alarmed, she said 'Why?'

'Do it! For a wager. It will help you understand how he felt – the recklessness, the madness! I tell you what – I'll wager all the books of my library. They could all be yours!'

She didn't trust him in this mood. He jumped up and leaned over the bench, his lean face transformed with feverish excitement. 'There's nothing like it! The thrill of knowing you could lose everything.'

'I haven't got anything to lose.'

'Of course you have!' He smiled, sidelong. 'You have what we all have. You have your soul.'

Sarah went cold.

The feeling she had had once before swept over her, of being balanced on the edge of a dark bottomless pit of terror, wobbling, unsteady.

'My soul?' she whispered.

'Yes.' Azrael looked eager. 'The most secret part of you. The real you. The spirit that will live for all eternity.'

He was joking, of course. And yet pictures from the old Bibles of the Library began to haunt her, the terrible screaming torments of the damned, who had chosen evil, burning, lost in unimaginable suffering. She turned to the table. 'That's not funny.'

'Indeed no. But consider. Does a person's soul even exist?'

'You should know. You're the alchemist.'

He smiled. 'I am. And science needs experiment. Why not find out? Go on Sarah. Turn the card.'

Slowly, she put her hand out. She looked down at the pack, their backs patterned with tiny chevrons that almost mesmerised her. The room was quiet. Outside the open window a few bats flitted under the eaves. The stars were bright and frosty.

She touched the cards.

The cat hunkered down, eyes wide. Far off in the stable, a horse whinnied. And she lifted her hand back, and closed it tight.

'Maybe I should go to church,' she said.

Azrael smiled.

NINE

Church was strange.

Azrael sat in the Trevelyan pew – she had never seen him there before. Darkly elegant, he listened to the sermon with scholarly reserve, raising an eyebrow now and then, or flicking a speck of dust off his knees, so that old Mr Martin the rector got flustered and lost his place in his notes.

In her new dress Sarah felt everyone was looking at her. Mrs Hubbard certainly was, over the rim of a gilt pince-nez, and behind her Major Fleetwood, his wife, and seven children, all identically dressed. Demure, Sarah smiled down at her gloves.

Over the chancel arch, there was a Doom painting. She had stared at it countless times before, but today it held her eyes as the doleful hymns of the service were sung, and the sea-fog dimmed the candles and made old men cough. On the left a hideous demon grimaced and capered; his black, tailed attendants forcing damned souls into the grinning mouth of a vast Hell; inside was all fire and torment. Small naked figures were being pulled out of their graves, wealthy and wailing, some with crowns, some with mitres, tearing their hair, wringing their hands. It reminded her of Azrael's strange eagerness over the cards. She'd heard stories from Martha about men who'd sold their souls. To the devil.

He hadn't been joking.

The fear she had felt swept back, and she fidgeted, dropped a glove and picked it up. And for a moment, as she glanced back up at the picture, she saw herself in it, a small white-faced creature half out of a grave, wailing, and her father and grandfather and all the faces from the paintings screaming silently around her, so that she froze in her seat, eyes widening slowly, the mists of sea fog obscuring the ancient plaster.

And then they were only small, indistinct sinners again, lost in disintegrating, flaking paint.

She shivered. On the right, things were better. She preferred this side. Just above Azrael's head the blessed spirits ascended, ranks of beautifully delicate winged angels in white, guiding the righteous up ladders. The top of the painting was long lost. Ghosts of figures loomed there, brilliant, barely seen.

Azrael caught her eye, and winked, darkly.

Mr Martin lost his place again.

'Are you sure?' Martha said anxiously. 'You really like it there?'

Sarah unpacked the fruit and cake and sweetmeats Azrael's cook had given her. 'Yes, I told you! It's fine! These are for papa. Don't tell him where they came from.'

'He'll know,' Martha said drily.

'How has he been?'

'Tormented.' The stout woman sighed, hitching the baby up on her hip. 'So fretful. Sits all day and says nothing. You'd best see for yourself, Sarah.'

Reluctant, she turned. Even after only a week at Darkwater the cottage depressed her. She saw now how dim and smoky and filthy it was, and she knew for the first time something of the despair her father must have felt, how heart-broken he and his young bride must have been, on that terrible day fifteen years ago. She stared at the row of cracked plates with loathing. She knew one thing already. She could never live here again. And suddenly she hated it that Martha had to live here, that all of them had to endure it, the squalid cottages, the boys with no shoes, the red raw hands of the fishwives, salt-swollen at the harbour. She hated it that they worked so hard, in the fields, down the mines, Jack out at sea for days, and all for so little. Martha could barely write her own name. And was proud of the cracked plates, because there were six, all matching.

It made Sarah despair. Because there was nothing she would ever be able to do.

For any of them.

Her father was sitting up in the meagre bed. He was reading an old newspaper, but he laid it down and looked at her coldly as she came in.

'New dress, I see. More than I could ever have bought you.'

She ignored it, and sat on the bed. He seemed weaker.

'How have you been, Papa?'

'As you'd expect. I exist, Sarah. I do not live. I think of you, up there. A servant in our house.'

She felt sure he was desperate to know all about it, but would never ask. She began to describe the wonders of the Library but he cut her short at once, angrily. 'Please. I have no desire to know the details of my destroyer's dissolute life.'

'He's not like that.' Sarah took an exasperated breath. 'He's quite likeable, really.'

'Indeed.' Her father coughed, painfully. 'You seem to have taken to his servitude easily enough. You obviously don't feel the shame of it. Still,' he waved a bone-frail hand and picked up the newspaper, 'that's to be expected. Your mother had no feeling for the family. You have always taken after her.'

White-faced with sudden fury she stood, hot tears prickling her eyes. She couldn't trust herself to say anything. Stalking past Martha she snatched her shawl and said, 'I'll be back next week.'

But she wondered if she would.

In Newhaven Cove the wind was whipping up a storm but she didn't care. It blew her hair all over and she let it. Tonight was All Hallows Eve. Tonight the wind would blow the ghost-ships to land, and all the spirits of the drowned would climb the cliffpath to the church. She watched the waves crash on barnacled rocks, spray flying as high as her own anger.

He was old. All the joy, all the excitement had withered out of him, so that all he could brood on were his misfortunes. She'd never be like that. She'd never let herself grow old. And it would go on until he died, because even twelve shillings all found wouldn't change things. He'd die in a damp bed in someone else's cottage, a man with no hope and nothing left but pride. There was nothing she could do about that, either.

Unless she really sold her soul to the devil.

Turning, tired with anger and a bitter grief, she came across footprints. They crossed the ridged beach, crisscrossed by wandering paws, rockpool to rockpool. She followed them, walking fast, but she had to scramble to the cliffbase before she found the tramp. He was sitting on a rock, gazing out to sea.

'Hello,' she said.

The tramp turned. His red, coarsened face broke into a toothless grin.

'Well, if it isn't the angry girl. Still angry too. Better dressed though, and a mite cleaner. Saw that in the chapel, I did.'

She sat by him, kicking sand from her boots. 'I didn't see you.'

'I was there. All watching thee, they were, the parish busies. And how is it, working for the Prince of Darkness?'

She laughed. 'Is that what they call him?'

' 'Tis what I call him. Don't thee trust him, mind. Not an inch. The devil incarnate, that one. Even his Hall built over a chasm that leads straight to Hell.'

Sarah forced down her fear. 'Rubbish. You don't know him.'

'Don't I?' The tramp stood up. 'That one and I go way back. I could tell ye things about him . . .'

'What things?'

The tramp studied her. 'How brave art thou?'

'Brave enough.'

'Aye?' He nodded, gravely. 'Well, look now. I'll be outside, in the Bear Garden, before dark. Don't come out after. Reckon you can get me summat to eat?'

She nodded, rubbing the dog's dirty fur.

'Well, bring it. And in return I'll tell thee some home truths about thy precious Lord Azrael.'

He shuffled off down the path towards Mamble. At the bend he turned, hitching up his belt of rope. 'Be careful. Don't tha make any agreement with him. No wagers, mind.'

For a long time, cold, ignoring the rain, she watched him go.

In the Library, Azrael was sitting at the telescope, preoccupied. Behind him Scrab fussed round with a feather duster.

As she took off her coat, she felt his dark eyes watching her.

'Sarah,' he asked quietly, 'who was that you were talking to?'

She turned, surprised; saw the lenscap was off, the brass tube tilted down. Scrab, now sweeping a burnt, twisted mass of glass off the floor, grinned to himself.

'Have you been watching me?' she snapped.

He looked abashed. 'It was accidental.'

'Oh, was it! Well you've got no right. I can talk to whoever I want!' Then she remembered he was her employer and took an angry breath. 'It was just some tramp, anyway.'

Azrael looked worried. He got up and wandered to the fireplace, crunching on the glass shards without noticing. Scrab scowled up at him, 'Watch yerself!'

'I don't want you to speak to him again,' Azrael said.

Sarah stared. Then she said 'Why not?'

He picked up a small glass globe and shook it, gently. Hundreds of tiny white snow-flakes swirled and drifted inside. 'He reminds me of someone I once knew. A troublemaker. A liar.' He looked at her sidelong. 'I don't want him on my land. I don't want you to speak to him.'

'You can't tell me who to speak to.'

71

He put the globe down, watching the flakes settle. Then he said, 'You work for me now, Sarah. Don't forget that.'

His face was troubled.

'You don't own me,' she said. 'Yet.'

But she knew a threat when she heard it.

TEN

The Bear Garden was cold. And so was she. The tramp was late.

She glanced up at the house, uneasy and defiant. After sitting in her room for an age telling herself not to be reckless, she'd grabbed the shawl, sped down through the kitchens and out into the smoky purple twilight. Maybe Azrael was afraid of what she'd find out.

The yew trees beyond the terrace were already black shapes, monstrous. Small statues of dancing bears capered on columns of stone higher than her head. She didn't like them, or their stony stillness. She kept thinking the one by the gate had turned its head to look at her.

An owl hooted in the wood.

Sarah paced restlessly up and down, trying to keep warm. Her breath smoked and the sky in the west was clouded. It must be getting late. She had no idea of the time; none of the clocks in Darkwater Hall ever worked, even though she'd wound the Library clock herself. Tonight was All Hallows Eve – the Night of the Dead. She didn't want to be out in it. If he didn't come now, she'd leave the food and go in.

There was candlelight in the Laboratory. As she glanced up at it she saw the window shutter's being closed; for a second she caught Scrab's stooped outline.

Then a stone rattled on the path.

The tramp was very quiet. He crept in through the

gate like a shadow, slightly breathless, the dog slinking
behind.

'That you, girlie?'

'Yes. Over here.'

She'd put the food on the bench in a little wicker
shelter she sometimes sat in; there were a few of them
round the gardens.

'There's none but us?' The tramp sounded wary.

'No.'

He came inside and sat down, smelling of woodsmoke
and onions. It was darker in here; she crouched by his
feet, wrapping the shawl tight about her shoulders to
keep warm. 'I've brought bread and potatoes and some
cheese. It's in the sack. Now tell me what you've got to
tell, and be quick.'

He rummaged in the dirty sacking, smiling his
toothless grin. 'Ah, yes. Tonight's that night, eh?'

She stared, struck by a thought. 'You won't sleep out
in it, will you?'

'I sleep where I like. On the beach, or His Lordship's
woods. Maybe a barn. Maybe the church porch.'

'But tonight . . .'

'Oh I've seen many a Hallow night.' He rubbed his
red, coarse face with a broad thumb. 'None of it ever
hurt me. But here,' he glanced round, uneasy, 'this is a
chancy place.' He nodded at the box hedges. 'Look at it.
No gardeners, not that you ever see. But the place is dug
and hoed and kept like a palace.'

Sarah nodded. 'I've noticed.'

'Servants in the house, is there?'

'Just a cook. And Scrab.'

'Ah!' The tramp shook his head. The name seemed to

alarm him. 'That feller! Summoned up from some hole under the furniture, him. Who needs servants when you can magic your own vermin?'

Taking out a piece of cheese he began to eat it, sucking at it in a way she found disgusting.

'Look, say what you came to say. He told me not to talk to you. He might send for me.'

The tramp's eyes were bright. 'He'll be too busy tonight. So he knows I'm here?'

'He saw us through the telescope.'

'He would.' He swallowed the cheese. 'I suppose he's got round thee. Has he told thee how he got this place?'

'He won it from my grandfather.'

'Aye. And I dare say he's full of remorse and wished to God it had never happened?'

'So he says.' Sarah felt unease grow inside her like the cold.

'You believe him?'

She shrugged. 'My grandfather was . . .'

'Thy granfer, girl, was a fool and braggart.' The tramp looked mournfully out at the darkening garden. 'And a good 'un.'

'You knew him?'

He gave a toothless wheeze. The dog yapped, and he caught its muzzle quickly with one hand. 'Loved him. Oftentimes he'd speak to me, riding by. He let me make hay and help with the shearing. "How's tricks, old villain," he'd roar, and then drink from the same cider-keg as all of us.'

'Azrael says,' Sarah pulled cobwebs off her dress, 'that he was cruel. That he didn't care for the people.'

The tramp glanced at her sidelong. 'His Lordship

should know about cruelty.' He took out a stinking old pipe and began to fill it with some peculiar weed. When he spoke again his voice was low. 'I was there, that night.'

She stared up at him. 'Where?'

'The Black Dog, out on the moor. I was sitting in the corner. Let me tell thee what really went on.'

The sky was dark now. Far down on the cliffs late kittiwakes gathered. The garden dimmed, minute by minute.

'Trevelyan was drunk. Azrael was buying. Strong stuff. Cider. Brandy. I watched how he poured it into thy granfer's tankard, filling again and again. The old man got worse and worse. That's the truth, girlie!'

Cold, she waited. He lit the pipe with a tinderbox, and puffed on it noisily. A tiny red ember glowed in the dark.

'I suppose he told thee different.'

'Yes.'

'Then tha'll have to choose who to believe. Anyway, they started the cards. Azrael's idea. He kept raising the stakes. Kept winning. Every hand turned out his way. The other players dropped out. One of them muttered he'd seen the black arts before, and wanted no part of it. Red as Hell it was, with the fire and all, and a strange crowd in there that night. Outside the wind was roaring, fit to burst.'

Sarah stood up. She knew what was coming. She walked to the doorway and stood with her back to him, staring tight-lipped at the dark garden. The bears watched her, peering over the hedges.

'It was Azrael,' the tramp said carefully, 'that made the last wager.'

'No!' She turned. 'My grandfather had a pistol . . .'

'No gun, girlie. "This time," Azrael says, all light and keen "we bet everything. House. Estate. Life. Even thy immortal soul, old man. On the turn of a card." He and thy granfer sat at that table as if they were only mortals left in Christendom. No one spoke. It was as if some dread lay on us. I remember the fire catching Azrael's face; dark it was, eager. I'll tell you this too, he's not changed. Not a line, not a wrinkle. In all these years.'

He puffed at the pipe. Sarah glared. 'Go on!'

'Nothing else to say. Trevelyan nodded, befuddled as he was. They drew the cards. Thy granfer's hand shook so much he could scarce cut the pack. He turned a King. We all knew how it would be though. How can you play with the Devil and win? When Azrael turned the Ace the whole room stopped breathing. Thy granfer just stood and staggered to the door. Holding himself stiff he was, his face as if he was already in Hell. The door crashed behind him. He never said a word.'

Sarah turned back to the garden, so he wouldn't see her dismay. She had no idea what to believe. In the darkness the columns seemed empty. 'Why would Azrael lie to me?'

'Why should I, eh? He's not like us. He's the Father of Lies.'

'Oh stop all that!' She stormed out on to the grass and turned on her heel to face him, quivering with anger. 'I know him! I don't know you!'

He was a dark outline. Only the pipe glowed, its redness rising and sinking with his breath. 'Take care with him.' The tramp stood, heavily. 'He's not brought thee here for any good purpose. Has he tried yet, to win thy soul?'

Fear shot through her.

'No. At least . . .' she shook her head. 'It was a sort of joke . . .'

'No joke, girlie. Not with Azrael. He'll try again. He'll offer thee anything tha wants, and in the end he'll win thee.'

He looked at her closely. 'Maybe he's won already.'

'Don't be stupid!'

'Then come with me now. I'll take thee home. To thy father.'

The tramp stepped forward. The dog barked, nervous.

She didn't know any more who she was angry with. She didn't know what to do. Bewildered, she saw suddenly that it was night, purple and mothy. The sun had long gone. It was All Hallows Eve.

'No,' she breathed.

'Tha must! Don't go back to the house, girlie! 'Tis what he wants!'

She thought of her father. The slovenly cottage. Cleaning the privies at the wretched school. And then all the books fell into her mind, the rows of chained, forbidden knowledge, and Azrael sitting by the fire feeding his cat with warm crumbs, saying, 'To change metal into gold, Sarah, think of that! Think of the wonder of that!'

The dog yelped, a sharp warning.

'I can't,' she muttered.

The garden crackled with movement. The bears had gone, as if they had slithered off their pillars; now she could hear a rustling all around her. Shadows merged into lithe shapes, panting, gathering.

The tramp swung the sack hastily over his shoulder. 'Come with me. The chance won't come again.'

'I can't.' She shook her head. 'I don't believe you.'

He looked at her, close. ' 'Tis worse than that. You do believe me. But you're still not coming.'

She couldn't answer.

Dogs howled. The uproar rang from the wood, and the tramp swore and plunged the cold pipe in his pocket. 'God help me,' he muttered 'I've heard that hell-sound before. Come on girlie, unless you want to suffer for all eternity!'

'Leave me alone! Just go!' she yelled, almost crying with fury. 'Quickly!'

He ran.

But from the wood the hounds were racing, black shapes lean and lolloping. The tramp crashed through the hedge, clanging the gate behind him. All the night was a sudden bedlam of noise, a breathless panting. As she stood rigid with terror the hounds came at her, streaming round, closing in, sniffing her dress, growling, a savage, spectral pack, tails upright. Cold rose from them, icy wisps of smoke. The red coals of their eyes burned into her. She felt sick, almost faint.

'Sarah!'

Azrael was coming. He rode over the lawn on his pale horse, forcing a way through. Reluctant, growling, the pack split before the trampling hooves; one dog leapt up at him and he kicked it down.

'Put your foot in the stirrup!' he yelled.

She reached up and grabbed; he pulled her quickly and she swung up behind him, clutching his coat.

Around them the hounds were a snarling blackness. Another growled and leapt up, its teeth snapping at her hand, and broke into a sudden earsplitting howl that made Sarah sure the horse would rear and throw them. But it snorted, and shook its head, and Azrael urged it on so that they galloped over the lawns, across the empty flowerbeds, up the steps to the door where Scrab waited in a swirl of mist and candlelight, all the shadow hounds streaming after them.

Breathless, Sarah jumped down.

'Go inside,' Azrael snapped.

The hounds were racing away. Far off in the woods the crashing pursuit brought rooks flapping out of the treetops like dark snow.

'Don't hurt him,' she whispered.

Azrael smiled. 'What do you think I am?'

Hopeless, she said, 'That's just it. I don't know what you are.'

He leaned down. 'Don't you? I warned you. I don't like trespassers. Now go in. This is Hallowe'en, remember?'

He turned the horse away, and she knew he had been laughing at her. She ran up the steps, fast.

In the wood the hounds erupted into a hoarse baying. They had found the scent. Someone yelled in terror.

She pushed past Scrab in fury.

'Get out of my way,' she muttered.

ELEVEN

November fell like a dark curtain.

Martha said there had never been such a Hallowe'en, not in living memory. Along the cliffs red fires had blazed – balefires the old men had called them, glimmering and gone. The wind had roared over slate-roofed cottages in the combes, and the villagers had barred the doors and huddled over the fires, listening and sleepless. 'Like all the hounds of Hell riding down the sky,' she said with relish, not noticing Sarah's stare.

Barns had blown down. One pinnacle of the church tower had crashed, found in the morning embedded point down in the soft earth of a recent grave.

There had been the usual sightings. John Trevisik swore he had seen his drowned brother looking in at the scullery window. At the inn at Mamble someone had rattled the doorhandle late at night and stumped angrily around, swearing and yelling. When the inkeeper had nervously unbarred a shutter and peered out, no one had been there.

Sarah had listened to it all in silence, her thumb scraping absently at a burn-mark on Martha's table. Jack came through. He stopped, awkward.

'How is it at the big house? You're looking well on it, Sarah.'

She knew that. She was clean, ate well, wasn't so scrawny. Her hair was well-brushed and shiny; she'd

81

bought another new dress and a finer pair of boots.

'I like it, Jack,' she said, not looking at him.

His open face clouded. 'Aye. I thought you would. We'll not be seeing you here much more.'

Her father asked no questions. Each time she saw him he seemed greyer, more discontented, his cough getting worse and worse. It upset her so much that last week she hadn't gone to see him at all.

On Hallowe'en, Azrael had been out all night.

In the morning he'd been tired but cheerful, perfectly polite. Scrab had told him he was a damned fool for wearing himself out. He had said nothing about the dark hounds and she wouldn't ask. But since then there had been no sign of the tramp. Nothing. In the village no one had seen him. It was as if he had disappeared from the face of the earth.

The weather turned colder. Withered leaves drifted down; woodsmoke rose from the orchards.

Sarah lived in a cosiness of rooms, of meals with Azrael, enthralled by his talk of astronomy, spirits, angels; his old tales and abstruse lore, speculations about the conjuring of demons, the possibility of mermen. He told her nothing about himself, easily changing the subject each time she asked. She worked hard. She took notes of all his experiments, learned strange chemical symbols, stayed up late to watch flasks of mysterious liquids change colour.

He fascinated her. Day by day she fell more under his quiet spell; the urgency of his desire for the secret of transmutation moving into her own mind, so that she lay awake at night thinking of mixtures of elements they hadn't tried, variations of heating and compression. And yet under it some fear of him lurked. He wanted her soul, the tramp had said. To damn it, or to save it? Or was he just crazy, a lonely man possessed with an impossible quest?

And all the time her father's cough seemed to rattle through her dreams.

Finally, one bleak afternoon in the Library, even the books were not enough. She dropped her pen, letting it blot, then leaned her arms on the open pages of dark print, resting her head on them.

She couldn't sit here. It was too silent. Not even a clock ticked in its dusty remoteness. She felt stifled, and suddenly, to her own surprise, she longed for Martha to talk to, or Jack, or even some of the children from the school. But, then, she'd made herself above them, just like she'd said she would.

Only it wasn't supposed to be like this.

She jumped up and stalked out, walking from room to room like a restless shadow.

Who was telling the truth – Azrael or the tramp? One of them was lying to her.

She wandered out of the Library wing and along the upper landings, recklessly throwing open all the doors. Bedrooms. Closets. A bathroom. All clean, well-kept. All empty.

She ran up the south stairs to the servants's attics and they were the same; small white rooms, neat in a row.

The terrible silence of the house oppressed her. Its statues seemed frozen, its paintings cruel and stern. The curtains hung absolutely rigid, as if a breeze had never touched them, as if the whole life of Darkwater was

83

suspended, like a chemical in solution, waiting for some explosion to happen. On impulse she dragged up the sash of a window, wrenching it open with all her strength. Cold wind gusted in, refreshing in its dampness, loud with the screams of gulls.

She leaned out, breathing the misty rain. All across the fields and out to sea grey curtains of it hung, veil beyond veil. It reminded her of something she had almost forgotten. Azrael's secret door. She had never found it.

She turned and walked past her own room to the tapestry at the corridor's end. Kneeling, she felt the corner again, this time with infinite care, jamming her fingernails into cracks and tugging hard. Nothing moved. There was no panel that she could find. Nothing. Except, as she turned away, something out of the corner of her eye, that she had to crouch down to see.

A few white spots of dried candlewax on the floor boards.

Sarah touched them, with a wry smile. They were tiny but quite hard, and they meant that someone had stood here for a few seconds, the candle askew and dripping in some draught. It was enough. She hadn't dreamed it. And if she could find out where the door led, it might help her know more about what or who Azrael was.

After a moment's thought she turned and marched down to the vast kitchens, where chickens turned on a spit under the sooty hearth, and Scrab sat at the table wrapping apples in sacking.

She stood right in front of him.

'Who is Azrael?' she demanded.

His small eyes looked at her in disgust. 'Yer master.'

He tossed another apple in the box.

'And where does he come from?'

He grinned then, the inflamed spots red under his greasy hair. 'Elsewhere. 'E's the one what 'olds all the cards.'

'Cards?' She caught at the word. 'What cards?'

Scrab scratched irritably. 'Restless today, ain't we! Flighty. And there was me thinking you 'ad all you ever wanted.'

Above him a bell jangled on the wall. LABORATORY was written under it in gilt letters.

Scrab didn't look up. 'Wants yer.' He tapped an apple so that a fat grub fell out, and he picked up the pale squashy thing in his fingers. As she went out, she was sure he was going to eat it.

Azrael was bent over the workbench, absorbed in the contents of a glass flask. He had been nervous and on edge all day. His expensive coat was stained with splashes.

'Do you know what this is?' he said at once.

'Acid?'

'Aqua Regis. It can dissolve gold.'

She came through the musty, cluttered room. 'And?'

'Sarah, I may finally have succeeded!' He gazed at her, pale with excitement. 'After all these lifetimes, Sarah! All this work! I started with the basest ingredients, but they've been purified and distilled, endlessly filtered, until now they're almost quite new, the faults strained and burned out. A painful process for them sometimes, I know, but we're so close!'

'Them?' she said, slowly. 'You sound as if you're talking about people. As if it's people you've been changing.'

He smiled, coy. 'Do I? Well, it's true the sages said that true gold is that which is created in the soul. The turning away from evil, from pride.'

'The soul again.'

'It's a subject that interests me.'

'The Trevelyans were proud,' she said. 'I wonder where their souls are.'

'Do you?' He held her gaze for a moment, then turned abruptly, 'Look,' he whispered.

She bent over the strange apparatus, sniffing its sour smell. The vessel was one Azrael called an alembic, and in the dish on the top was a tiny crust of brass-coloured metal, cold and brittle.

'Is that gold?'

'I pray so.' He seemed too nervous to keep still; putting the flask down he paced over to the fireplace and put both hands to it, leaning on the marble mantelshelf. Looking down into the fire made his face a mask of shadows and red light. 'Whether it is or not, is up to you.'

'Me!'

'Pour the Aqua Regis on to it. Carefully. If it dissolves, its gold. I will have done what generations have only dreamed of.'

He was watching her intently in the mirror. The cat was staring too, its green eyes tense. Sarah shrugged and picked up the flask, oddly uneasy. Outside, the rain pattered on the windows.

But just as she went to pour he said, 'First. Is there anything . . . you want?'

She looked at him. 'I've got everything I want.'

'Are you sure? Think hard Sarah. Think of your father.

Of Martha, of all the villagers. Think what you could do for them.'

The flask was heavy. Her hand trembled.

Azrael stepped forward. 'We could make an agreement,' he whispered.

But instead of answering she asked a question. 'What happened to the tramp?'

'Who?'

'The tramp. You know.'

'He ran off.' He seemed irritated. 'Never mind him! Please Sarah . . .'

'He told me things. He said you deliberately destroyed my grandfather.'

Azrael's gaze went dark. 'Indeed.' For a moment he was silent, watching her. 'And you believe him?'

'I don't know who to believe.'

'He's not the first to make such claims,' Azrael said sadly. 'I have always been misunderstood. But I told you what really happened.'

'And he warned me.'

The cat spat. Azrael turned. 'Warned you?'

'Not to make any bargains with you.'

He shook his head, his smile hard. 'You already have. You work for me.'

Sarah's fingers were tight around the smooth glass. 'I know.'

'And you really think I would ruin your family? For what?' He waved a hand. 'For this? I have estates of my own, Sarah.'

'So you keep saying. But I don't know anything about you. And you've got too many things that should be mine.'

She looked at the flask, then put it down on the table, quickly. 'I'm sorry. I can't. I think you'd better do this yourself.'

She walked to the door, and glanced back. Azrael had picked up the flask. All the excitement seemed to have drained right out of him. Bitterly he poured out one drop of acid.

The crust of metal stayed exactly as before.

She turned and went out. She didn't want to see his disappointment.

That night she waited in the Library, reading. She read feverishly, as if all the words of all the people from the books could block out the loneliness she felt. She should never have come here. But it was too late now. She was changed. She could never bear to go home, not back to the cottage. Because this was home. Every day she felt that more strongly. It was so easy to wander the empty house and feel that it was hers. That was the thought that kept intruding, round the edges of the words.

Turning a page, she heard a door creak.

She looked up.

Footsteps walked stealthily down the corridor.

At last!

She slid to her feet; opening the library door she saw Azrael at once in the shadows of the landing. He was climbing the south stairs quickly, the cat a lithe slither at his feet. She slipped out, silently.

Above her, on the walls, his candle threw bizarre shadows. They moved around him like a host of attendant spirits, the cat streaking ahead.

Keeping well back, determined, Sarah followed him.

She slid from doorway to doorway, lurking behind great vases. On the stairs she tiptoed on the crimson carpet.

She knew where he was going. Down the dim corridor past her bedroom, the cat sniffing at the closed door. Azrael's shadow stretched long and eerily over the panelled wood. Then he stopped.

Crushed in an alcove, her fingers tight on a velvet curtain, she watched, intent.

Azrael pulled the tapestry aside. He lifted the candle and she saw only the wall, but he touched some part of it and the whole panel seemed to spring forward, and she saw it really was a door, ingeniously hidden. He drew out a bunch of keys; they clinked in the silence.

After one quick look down the corridor he unlocked the door and went through, leaving it ajar. For a long moment she waited, seeing again the weird red glow that flickered through the slit, and then she moved swiftly after him, slipping through the tapestry folds and easing the door wide.

There were stairs, going down.

She had to be careful; after a while tiny stones scattered under her feet. The stairs were stone, and crumbling. They made a great curve, and she tiptoed down and down until she felt sure she was below the cellars, below the house itself, and still the steps descended and far down ahead of her the roar and grumble of the Darkwater grew loud. It echoed, as if there were caves down there, and the strange misty glow in the air was a steamy heat, and the stench of some powerful sulphurous miasma came up to her.

Ahead, far down, Azrael's dark shape turned a last knob of rock. She lingered, waiting in tense excitement, seeing how a sudden redness lit him, as if huge fires burned down there.

And then a voice in her ear said slyly, 'I'm glad yer still up, Miss Nosy. There's someone here to see yer.'

Azrael turned. In the echoing roar he stared up at her and his face was a dark amazement and then a fury that chilled her.

'Get her out!' he hissed, and Scrab grabbed her hand and pulled her hastily up the stairs, an endless scrambling breathless climb until they tumbled out into the corridor hot and trembling.

In seconds Azrael was with them. He slammed the door and locked it and turned on her in wrath. 'You were following me! Why, Sarah?'

'Because you never explain anything to me!'

Scrab was waving someone down the corridor.

'I can't,' Azrael said tightly. 'Not yet.'

'Sarah?' It was Martha, wet through, almost distraught. She glanced at Azrael in fright, then grabbed Sarah's hands. 'You have to come home . . .'

'No!'

'You must!' Martha gripped tighter. 'Right now Sarah. Your father's dying.'

TWELVE

The fire spat, but still the cottage was cold.

Pulling her woollen shawl tighter, Sarah propped a few more sticks on the flames and then the last of the sea-coal, kneeling on the old rag rug with the holes in it.

Under blankets, her father coughed.

They had brought his bed into the kitchen, nearer the warmth, but it was still far too draughty. She could feel the raw wind whistling and gusting in all the chinks, and the back door had rattled and banged all night. One tiny rushlight guttered on the table.

'Sarah.'

She hurried over. 'Papa? I'm here.'

'A drink. Please.'

She poured the water and held it to his dry lips. He sipped it, one hand frail as a claw holding on to her wrist. When he leaned back he was sweating, despite the chill, his breath caught like a fluttering bird in his throat.

He gasped, 'She should never have fetched you.'

'Don't be silly.'

'You have your new life now, away from this . . . slum.'

Even now, she thought, he was bitter. She sat on the rough blanket; he looked away, restless. Despite his sunken cheeks his white hair made him look more lordly than ever. For a second she imagined him warm and safe in Azrael's sitting room, his feet on the footstool, the

91

porcelain tea-service on the table. It was where he ought to be.

'Listen,' she said, almost angrily. 'You must come back to Darkwater with me. The doctor says there's every chance of a good recovery if you had . . .'

'I will never set foot in that place. Not while he's there.'

She knotted the ends of the shawl. Then she said, 'What if he wasn't there?'

He turned, his chest rising with the effort of breathing. 'What?'

'If he wasn't there. If he'd gone. Would you come then?'

Driftwood crackled and spat.

Her father drew himself up, a pitiful, stubborn effort. 'Sarah. I will not enter the Hall unless this . . . interloper admits it was never his in the first place. Unless he restores what is ours with every apology. Legally.' He slumped back, suddenly grey. 'And that he will never do.'

He coughed, and she helped him up, feeling the tension knotted in his frail shoulders, the sickening knowledge of his ruin, that he never allowed to leave him. It was a while before she spoke again.

'Papa. Was your father as cruel a man as people say?'

Surprised, he stared at her, the gold silk of the dressing gown dirty at his neck. 'Cruel? He was firm. He had to be.'

'He evicted families who couldn't pay. Killed a man.'

Impatient, he shook his head. 'The people here are weak, my girl. Feckless. Living among them, I can see that even more clearly. For centuries the Trevelyans were the only law in these counties. We had to take the lead.

Stand no nonsense. Generation after generation, we had to commit the criminals to the gallows and uphold the rights of property. If they hated us for it, it was the price we paid. But we too, we're getting weaker. Just like all the rest.'

His voice was a whisper.

'Or being purified,' she said.

'What?'

'Nothing. Something Azrael said. Go to sleep now.'

He lay looking up at her, uncertain, suddenly childish. 'If I do, will you still be here?'

She picked up his thin hand. 'Yes. Till the morning.'

The carriage was waiting.

How Azrael had known when to send it she didn't know, and she didn't recognize the coachman either, but she climbed wearily in and slammed the door, pulling the window blinds down.

The horses snorted, moving off with a jolt and a chink of harness. For a while she sat there, too tired to think and yet feeling remote and grand. She knew she enjoyed feeling that.

They clattered noisily through the village, through the first swirls of snow that spun from the bleak dawn sky, and in the cold creaky darkness she leaned forward and lifted one corner of the blind. She saw how the village women plucked their children anxiously away from the coach; how the wheels splashed the fishermen working at their nets. They scowled and swore. How did they feel about Azrael? She knew they had stupid, superstitious ideas, but it struck her now that he was a good landlord, generous to his tenants. No one had been turned out because they couldn't pay. It was more than her family had ever done.

She was so tired. Rubbing her face with her hands was no help. She was shivering now, and the fast rattle and jolt of the coach made her feel sick, until the crunching under the wheels went suddenly smooth and she knew they were racing up the long rutted curve of the drive.

She pulled up one blind.

The morning was grey. Darkwater Hall rose up through the gusts of snow like a fortress from some old gothic manuscript, and as the coach swept round she saw how the gargoyles spat and snarled in their ferocious stillness, a silent malice.

Jumping out, she ran up the steps, snow stinging her cheeks. Scrab had the door open. 'Thought you'd be back,' he jeered.

She ignored him and ran, up the great stairs, under the portraits of her long dead family, along the corridor, through the whole Library wing, setting all her carefully ordered stacks of catalogued papers fluttering and spilling in a sudden draught.

Then she flung open the door.

Azrael was looking in the wall safe. It was empty.

'Where's the jar?' she asked, breathless.

'Jar?'

'With the two boys inside.'

'Ah.' He locked the safe. 'That will come later. Now, how is your father?'

'Worse.' She came over and picked up a small crucible, looking at its fine cracks and seeing nothing.

'All right,' she said. 'You win.'

'Win?'

'Yes. I'll make your agreement.'

He sat down, smiling a little in surprise. 'I see. This makes me very happy, Sarah.'

Clumsy, she turned the crucible in her cold fingers and it fell, smashing into white porcelain slivers with a crash that made her heart leap. 'I'm sorry.'

'It's nothing.' Azrael touched the remains with his foot. 'Scrab will clean it up. Give him something to do. But Sarah, you should not be so nervous.'

'I'm not,' she snapped.

He nodded. 'So. Tell me what you want.'

She took a deep breath. 'I don't know who – what – you are. I do know you have power, over our lives, over the way things happen. I want my father to come back here, back to his home, and he won't unless the estate is ours again. I want you to give us back the estate.'

For a moment she expected him to laugh, but his smile was wry and grave. 'I see. And, on your side . . . ?'

'A promise. That things will be different. That we'll make up for the past. We'll treat the people fairly, I swear we will.'

'You might. But your father?'

'My father has learned his lesson.'

'Indeed?' Azrael looked politely dubious. 'What I see is a man who never leaves the cottage. Who lets his sixteen-year old daughter do the work he cannot bear to think of. Does he love you more for what you do for him, Sarah, or is he secretly ashamed of you? Or of himself?'

She looked at him. 'That's not fair!'

'Maybe not. But your father. Tell me Sarah, has he

95

even been humbled? Has living for fifteen years in a slum made him more sympathetic to the poor, feel more for their terrible struggle? Will he be generous with the wealth of Darkwater? Or will he just gorge himself on comforts, spend on luxury, make up for lost time? Will he even remember the Marthas and the Emmelines?'

She shrugged, miserable.

'Yes.' Azrael kicked the fragments sadly. 'I think you know the answer to that as well as I. How can I give the tenants another selfish master, just to please you?'

The silence was intense. Into it she said, 'I have something else I can offer.'

'And that is?'

He was waiting for her to say it. So she said it, harshly. Squashing down her fear, telling herself he was mad.

'My soul.'

Azrael gave the smallest of sighs. He limped to the window and leaned on the gleaming brass of the telescope. She could almost sense his pleasure.

'My father will die . . .' She took one step after him. 'Unless he comes back.'

Azrael gazed out at the wintry sea. 'Have I treated you well?' he asked softly.

Surprised, she said 'You know you have.'

'Then I won't fail you now. But—' he held up his hand as she came forward. 'There are conditions. These things have rules. You have to work for it. How long do you think it would take to make up for the oppression of centuries?'

She laughed, scornful. 'Another hundred years might do it.'

He nodded. 'You think I'm making fun of you. But a

hundred years it is. You have the estate for that time. Use it well, Sarah. At the end of the time I will come for your soul.'

The room was utterly silent.

She stared at him, at his grave dark face with its neat beard, a cold unease like a thread of ice inside her. For a moment she knew with certainty that he was some vast, eternal power. And then she knew he was a madman, and felt utterly stupid. 'You really believe that,' she whispered.

'Humour me.' He went to the desk, took a sheet of paper and a pen and began to write, the swift, sloping writing she knew so well. As she watched she rubbed sore eyes, bewildered.

'You're tired,' he said, without looking up.

'I stayed up with Papa all night.'

'Scrab will bring us breakfast. And then you should sleep.' He came over. 'After you've signed this.'

It was written in red ink and sealed. It said,

I, Sarah Trevelyan, the undersigned, hereby accept from the hand of the lord Azrael the freehold and properties of Darkwater Hall from this day forward for the period of one hundred years. In return I pledge to him the eternal possession of my immortal soul.

'This is stupid,' she said, terrified and confused. 'I just want . . .'

'Sign it.' He put the pen in her hand. 'Trust me, Sarah.' The room was chill. Snow clogged the sills. The door creaked as the cat slid in.

'I just want to bring my father home,' she muttered.

'I know that. Sign it.'

'The cottage is too cold for him! He wasn't brought up to it.' He took her hand and guided it to the paper.

'There. Just your name.'

'And you'll really go?'

'The Hall will be his. Legally. If you sign.'

She shook her head, unbearably weary, and laughed an exasperated laugh. 'I don't know what to make of you. I think we must both be mad.'

'If we are it doesn't matter,' Azrael said.

So she put the paper on the bench and signed it.

Sarah Trevelyan

THIRTEEN

At once all the clocks had started ticking.

Lying in bed now, shivering under the heavy covers, she remembered that, and it seemed to her as if the house had woken up at that precise moment, that the windows had begun to rattle and the boards creaked, as if far below the Darkwater raging through its underground caverns had roared with a strange fury. Even lying here now, barely awake, she could hear tiny movements that had not been in the house before, gusts and the bang of a door, the rapid scuttle of a beetle across some wainscot.

It took her a long time to fall asleep.

When she did, her dreams were a jumble. She found herself in a room full of clocks, their ticking so loud she put her hands to her ears, staring round. It was the Laboratory. But Azrael's experiments had dust all over them, the alembics cracked, the liquids and chemicals in every tube dried and crusted.

'Where are you?' she called.

There was someone standing by the mechanical model of the planets. A dark man, shadowed by the heavy curtains. As she watched he set the model moving, and the planets spun off their wires and went careering round the room, whizzing past her. She had to duck, feeling their fiery glow, the ends of her hair singed by Mercury's sizzle.

'Stop it!' she hissed. 'You're breaking it!'

It wasn't Azrael. It was the tramp. He stepped out of shadow and she saw how big he was, taller and broader than she remembered, his coat tied with string looking more like a belted robe, and a great sword in his hand.

'Tha's done it now, ain't thee!' he said angrily. 'Tha's made the pact with him!'

'I had to. I had no choice!'

'There's always a choice!' he roared. 'Thou'rt lost now, girl! Lost for ever and all eternity!' And he swung with his sword, and the glass vessels crashed and tinkled, the top of the bench cleared with one terrible sweep, a thousand fragments bouncing and shattering on the floor.

'This too,' he raged, and she jumped aside as he shoved the telescope over and dragged everything off the mantelshelf, notes, papers, books, carvings, globes, and hurled them all into the fire.

The fire! She had never seen it so huge; it snarled and crackled and spat like something alive. She was almost sure she could see hands in it, tiny red hands that grasped and seared and curled the paper, a demonic delight in the roaring and heat. It had spilled out of the grate; now it rampaged through the Laboratory, devouring benches and tables and in the heart of the smoke the tramp was unlocking the wall safe with a great black key.

'Come on,' he yelled to her. 'This way!'

There was a glass jar inside, and with another key he opened a tiny door in its side and grabbed her hands and pulled her in, the fire laughing hoarsely behind them.

The room was a strange one. There was a bed in it, and the odd lamp she had seen before, and a box-like contraption and small, cheap-looking furniture. All its colours were bright. On the walls huge coloured pictures of men in ridiculously short trousers with numbers on their garish shirts shocked her. They were photographs. She was amazed at their colour, at how real they looked.

The twins were there. One lay on the bed, the other sat by the window, looking out. He was talking.

'I would have died if it hadn't been for you,' he was saying.

Sarah was alone; the tramp had vanished. Now the twin on the bed sat slowly up. He was staring at her.

'Tom,' he said softly. 'She's back.'

Tom turned. They were identical, both about her age. 'I can't see anyone.'

'She's here.' The other boy stood. There was something misty in his outline. He blurred as he reached out to touch her, and she twisted away with a hiss of fear as his hand became the paw of a black cat, soft on her fingers.

Then, a long time later, she was dreaming of the beach. It was grey and raining, and the gulls screamed over her head. Azrael sat on a rock, elegantly, as if it was a throne. He wore his dark expensive coat, and behind him stood a huge grandfather clock – the one from the Oak Dining Room – and it ticked, but its tick wasn't mechanical, it was a human voice, infinitely weary, repeating the same words over and over. 'Tick. Tock. Tick. Tock.'

She stepped nearer. 'Is that . . . ?'

Azrael smiled, sadly. 'Your grandfather, I'm afraid. Doomed to be trapped in eternal torment. Until of course, your actions release him. Oh, and your father. Do you want to see him?'

'Yes,' she breathed.

The rain drifted apart. She saw him lying on the sofa

in Darkwater Hall, wrapped warmly in cashmere and wool. A great fire blazed in the grate. He poured tea into a vast porcelain cup.

Azrael came over to her. 'You'll see. It will be worth it.' He put a small card into her hand. 'But I will come for you, Sarah. Wherever you go, wherever you think you can run, there'll be no escaping me. No one ever does. The experiment has to run to the end.'

The mist closed round him. A small beetle ran into a hole in the sand.

She turned. Mrs Hubbard put the cane into her hand. 'You're a menial!' She took a huge pinch of snuff out of an open desk. 'What are you?'

Silent, Sarah watched the cane. It grew a tail, and back legs.

'What are you?' Mrs Hubbard snapped, ominously.

Front paws. A great head, its jaws wet and slobbering, growling, the red eyes opening, nostrils fuming with smoke, and as she turned it sprang on her and she screamed, and yelled, 'A menial!'

Sarah opened her eyes.

She was soaked with sweat. The fire was out, a grey gather of ashes, and through the curtains the dimness of a winter afternoon filtered.

She sat up, dressed in a furious rush, and ran down the stairs.

The Servants' Hall was empty. Here too, the fire was out. There was no sign of the cook and nothing to eat; she picked up some bread from the table but it was stale, rock hard. Annoyed, she flung it at the ashes.

'Scrab!' she yelled.

No one answered.

The Library was a mess. Somehow the wind had got in and whipped everything out of order; it would take days just to sort it out. Dumping armfuls of pamphlets on the desk she marched through to the Laboratory, and flung the door open.

The room was completely empty.

She stared in disbelief. It was all gone, the benches, alembics, astrolabes, boxes, charts. The walls were bare. Even the telescope had gone. All she saw was a dusty space, with an old clock ticking on the mantelshelf and the curtains thick with cobwebs. As if none of it had ever been here at all.

'Azrael?' she whispered.

A cold fear moved inside her, a sickening emptiness in her stomach.

She turned and ran out, into other rooms. Everywhere it was the same. The house was deserted. And more than that, it was transformed. Time had come back. Decay had resumed. It was a palace festooned with webs, the doors warped from long neglect, the Trevelyan portraits lost under grime. In the hall the black and white tiles were cracked, choked with leafdust and melted snow that gusted under the door.

Her face white, she went into the drawing-room.

It was cold. Through the tall windows she could see nothing but snow, swirling in silent cacophonies of storm outside. Far out in it the sun was setting, a sliver of scarlet into the invisible sea.

The piano was covered in dust. On Azrael's footstool a small white card was pinned. She pulled it off, quickly.

ALL YOU WANT IS YOURS. MY SOLICITORS

WILL SORT OUT THE LEGAL PROBLEMS. BE
GENEROUS. ON THE LAST STROKE OF THE
CLOCK ON THE LAST NIGHT OF THE YEAR IN
ONE HUNDRED YEARS LOOK FOR ME.

He hadn't signed it.

Folding the corner over in her fingers she looked
round, bewildered. She had done it. She had the house.
Her father could come home. Azrael had gone.

It must be some sort of mania, she told herself. All his
studying, all those years of guilt and disappointment, all
that medieval nonsense about spirits and elements and
demons had deranged him. She should have seen it
before. Everyone else had.

But as she stood there in the empty house all she
could hear in the silence were the clocks, ticking.

They had never seemed so loud.

THE GREAT WORK

FOURTEEN

It was his bedroom all right, but something had happened to it.

For a start, all the walls had turned to glass.

Tom sat up in the bed, swung his feet out and whispered 'Simon!'

No answer.

Pulling the bedclothes back he saw his brother's warm empty place. Tom got up, crossing the worn carpet. Carefully, he reached his hands out and felt for the invisible wall and it was there, behind the football posters, smooth and cold and curving in slightly as it rose. Like a dome. Or a jar. Even standing on the bed he couldn't reach the ceiling.

Outside it was dark. Vast dim shapes moved, spheres and planets, an enormous far-off door opening and closing, and then the sudden nightmare swelling of a great whiskered cat, that made him crumple back with terror against the pillow. The creature's vast soft mouth and nose were pressed against the glass. It mewed, its rough pink tongue rasping hopelessly, so close he could see the tiny hooks on it. Wide green eyes watched him.

Then it was gone.

After a second, pyjamas drenched with sweat, he said, 'Simon. Please. I need you.'

Something large and dark swished outside, and he ducked. Sounds came to him, distorted and filtered, of footsteps and a distant roaring that might have been water. And voices, asking some question.

Scared, he plugged the lamp in quickly and switched it on, and Simon sat up in the bed, tousled and sleepy.

'What's going on?'

'I don't know. I think this is a dream.'

Simon stared over his shoulder, eyes widening. 'Look!'

But Tom could see her. Her face was huge, an enormous pitted surface of skin, vast nostrils, stretched eyes. Her breath misted the glass. With a yell he leapt away, and the room shook; it toppled over and fell and plummeted into darkness, a huge warm darkness and—

A heart was beating.

Loud. Really loud.

It was thumping all round him, and he and Simon were tiny, lying close, curled in its rhythm, in a red landscape of tunnels and caves and hollows, veins and womb, all breathing, rising and falling. Beside him then he felt his brother's warm, empty place.

And the jar was falling; he was tumbled roughly, buffeted against its sides, great hands clasping him, pulling him out into the terrible light, a light that made him scream, and the huge face said, 'One's alive, doctor. Just the one.'

He sat up, sweating. 'Simon?'

His brother was on the windowseat, reading a football magazine. 'At last,' he said, without looking up. 'You'd better get up. Mam's been calling you.'

Of all places, it would have to be the Post Office. Tom chewed his toast and looked down at the parcel in cold despair. 'Now?'

'Well the post goes at ten. And when you've sent it, come up to the Hall and I'll get the new caretaker to sign you on for a few hours work, if you want. I'm desperate for the help, Tom.'

His mother took the tray out to the kitchen, and Tom shoved the parcel between the cereal box and the sugar bowl, and ran his hands through his hair in terror. 'Oh God. Not there,' he whispered.

Simon was lounging on the sofa. 'It's all right. We'll be quick. And he might not even be there.'

'He'll be there.'

It was Steve Tate he was afraid of. Steve's dad kept the Post Office, and Steve helped there in the holidays. Or rather, he loitered around the till drinking lager with his mates. Little Mark Owen, the sneaky one. And Rob Trevisik, big and thick. Tom dreaded them all. He never, ever went near the place.

His mother came back, rolling her overall into a plastic bag. 'Don't forget. Pound of potatoes. Margarine. And the parcel.'

'Can't you drop that in?' he asked, too casually.

'Tom, I'm late as it is. You'll come to the Hall after?'

He shrugged, appalled. 'Nothing better to do.'

Paula kissed him on the head, not listening. 'Good. Think of the three quid an hour.'

She went out. They heard her wheel the bicycle out of the shed. Then Simon stirred. 'Come on, lazy.'

Tom scowled at him. He cleared the table and dumped the dishes in the sink, seeing his own double reflection in the shiny taps, his face twisted and scared. As the hot water gushed out he thought that his mother never noticed when he was being sarcastic. He had plenty of things to do. Course work for one.

While he washed up Simon vanished, only coming in through the back door as the last plate was dried.

'It's raining. Hard.'

Tom glanced at him. Today his brother wore expensive jeans and a green sweatshirt and had his hair slicked down in the way Tom secretly wanted his. He looked tall and confident. There wasn't a drop of rain on him. But then, there wouldn't be.

Tom pulled a coat on and shoved the parcel in his pocket. 'Are you coming?' he asked, into the mirror.

Simon came up behind him, and he turned, facing again the wonder of his own face saying things he wasn't saying, thinking what he couldn't think. His brother said awkwardly, 'Look Tom. You know it's up to you. Keep strong, or I can't help.'

The rain was heavy. It poured off the cottage porch, soaking him as he went through it, and all the stone walls of the lane gleamed granite-grey. The sea was invisible in squalls and cloud, but the gulls were raucous, screaming and mewling over the far cliffs. Tom pulled his hood up and trudged, jumping puddles, past the caravan park to the stile in Martinmas Lane. A few expensive-looking mobile homes were still there, locked up for the winter. Underneath one, a child's pushchair with one wheel missing lay forlornly. Tom climbed over the stile and saw Darkwater Hall.

In the November rain, shrouded with ivy, it looked like some house out of an old Cornish tale of smugglers, demons and squires, all gothic windows and gargoyles. People said the devil had lived there once, and that under it he had dug a tunnel that led straight down to Hell.

'Daft.' Simon sat on a wall. 'It's a natural chasm in the rock.'

'I know that.'

'It's just you prefer the other yarn.'

They grinned an identical grin, but glancing back Tom's face darkened. Darkwater may look like some lord's house, but it wasn't. It was a school. A really good school. But he didn't go to it. His mother was just the cleaner.

'You'll miss the post,' Simon muttered.

Tom didn't move. Outside the Hall a taxi had pulled up, a sleek black one. A man was getting out. He was tall, darkhaired and wore a long black coat. The driver came round and opened the car boot, dumping two suitcases ungraciously on the steps of the Hall, and the tall man paid him. But he didn't ring the bell. Instead he stepped back and looked up at the building, a long look, with something of reminiscence about it. Then he turned, looking up at Tom, high on the cliffs, curiously. He wore a neat dark beard.

Tom jumped down.

'New teacher,' he said, sourly.

Then he ran. Down the lane, the wet umbels and ferns soaking his boots, past the School Cottage and the converted Art Gallery and the craft shops, racing past the garage and round to the Post Office with its front stacked with Christmas trees, freshly cut.

He stopped dead, feeling Simon thump into his back.

'Well. They're here.'

Outside, among the fir branches, two bicycles leaned.

111

FIFTEEN

For five minutes he sweated and prowled among the houses, sick with fear. Finally, with a great effort, he managed to get himself to the door and turn the handle. There was a bell on the door; it jangled.

The shop smelt of Christmas trees, polish, cabbages, chewing gum. Its fluorescent lights flickered and hummed.

Steve Tate was lounging by the till. The other two were leaning over some magazine, giggling, until the small one, Mark, looked up and nudged his mates. Instantly Steve was on his feet. 'Well! Look who's crawled in. Little Tom Thumb.'

The name hit Tom like a blow. They'd called him that since they were all kids. He'd been small then; he wasn't now. But they knew how much he hated it.

'Shut up,' he muttered.

It was a mistake. Steve went wide-eyed. 'Touchy, isn't he?'

Mark grinned and the big one, Rob, came over and blocked the way through the shop.

'Can we help you?' he asked, sarcastically.

Tom's heart sank. He glanced past. The Post Office counter was empty; he could hear Steve's dad rummaging for something in the storeroom at the back. Simon had vanished. He was on his own.

'No. Thanks.' He even felt small; his whole self

shrivelling up inside. His voice went tight and scared. He hated himself for trying to sound friendly. 'I've just got to get this posted, that's all.'

He stepped to one side; Rob stepped with him, as if in some ludicrous dance.

'I'll weigh it for you,' he said.

Instantly he had snatched the parcel, tossed it to Steve. Tom swung round, despairing. 'Be careful!'

'Why? Fragile is it? Watch it Mark, it's fragile.' Steve juggled the small box from hand to hand, then threw it to Mark who only just caught it, slamming back into a shelf of tins and sending a few rolling down the aisle.

Tom felt sick, though he knew there was nothing breakable in the box. Hot and humiliated his mind groped miserably after Simon, but there was no one there.

'Come on,' he said, managing a weak smile. 'Let's have it.'

'Did you hear that?' Steve came out from behind the counter. 'He's asking for it, boys.'

Tom froze. Cold chilled his back. The other two were idiots but Steve was worse. Dangerous. Unpredictable. Years ago, just for the hell of it, he'd pushed Tom down the old tin shaft out on the moor. The terror of that fall flashed over him now, the black sludge, his head bleeding, the way he'd curled in the corner and sobbed. He'd been lucky not to have broken his back.

That was then. He raised his head and looked at Steve's eyes. They were pale blue and cold. He was grinning.

'Not like you to come in here, Tom. Thought you were too keen on the old schoolbooks. Think yourself a bit above us, don't you.'

'Don't be stupid.'

The shop door clanged. A blonde girl with a rucksack came in and looked at them. Then she went round to the groceries. Tom almost let the relief show.

Steve stepped closer. 'Like those snobs up at the Hall. Bet you'd like it up there, Tommy. Pity your mother's just the cleaner.'

Rob snorted. But the door at the back opened and Mr Tate came in. 'Right. Who's next?'

There was silence.

Then Steve took the parcel and threw it back to Tom. 'He is.' He came up and rumpled Tom's hair and whispered in his ear. 'See you later, bright boy.'

Tom pushed past. It was better to say nothing. Dumping the hated parcel on the scales he pulled out some money and counted the slithering coins out blindly, feeling his face heat up as if it was swollen or had been slapped.

'One sixty.' Mr Tate tore stamps out of the book.

Tom glanced in the convex mirror, nervous. The girl was watching him. Behind the rows of soup and baked beans she was watching his back thoughtfully, and then she turned and took four tins to the shop counter. 'Do you cut keys?' she asked.

Carelessly jabbing the till buttons, Steve nodded.

'Thanks.' Tom shoved the parcel under and headed for the shop counter quickly. He had to get the rest of the stuff while there were people here. But to his despair he saw Steve's dad glance round and go back outside.

Grabbing the potatoes and some margarine from the fridge he dumped it hastily next to the girl's tins. She glanced at him, a quick glance as she took a note from a

114

small velvet purse. But she'd go, wouldn't she. And he'd be left with them. Steve was already counting her change. Tom felt Rob come close behind him. Something tapped him on the back of the head.

The girl put the tins in her rucksack. Then she swung it on to her back and put her hands in her pockets. She took out a pair of blue woollen gloves and pulled them on. Slowly.

Tom slapped his money down. Straightfaced, Steve punched the till buttons, then tutted. 'Oh dear. Done it wrong.' He smiled. 'Bear with me.'

His back wet with sweat, Tom gave the girl a quick glance. She looked away, and put her hands in her pockets.

But she didn't go.

Steve stared at her. 'Anything else?'

The girl eyed him. She was their age, but her look had a straight confidence. 'I'm waiting for him. Hurry up and serve him.'

Steve's surprise turned to instant mockery. 'Fancy him do you? Didn't know you had it in you, Tommy.'

Tom pushed the money at him, grabbed the potatoes and said, 'Keep the change.' He was desperate to get out but the girl said, 'Oh no. You give him his change. Come on.'

The cash drawer sprang open. Steve glared at it. He pretended to pick up coins but the girl said, 'Stop fooling about. Bit of a prat really, aren't you.'

Tom went cold.

Steve looked at her, and put the pound coin deliberately on the newspapers. 'You'll wish you hadn't said that,' he whispered.

She smiled. 'I'm terrified.'

'Come on.' Tom lunged for the door and dragged it open, the bell clanging. Cold wet air engulfed him like a welcome; he ran into it, down the steps, chilled with sweat.

The girl followed more slowly. She walked after him round the corner and found him leaning against the wall of the garage, breathing hard. 'You shouldn't let them mess you around.'

He stared down the lane. 'I don't.'

'Liar. I could see.'

'I can handle them. They were just . . .'

'They crushed you. Made you feel like nothing.' She pushed her short, bleached hair behind one ear. 'You have to face them down.'

'That's easy for you to say,' he breathed, furious.

She looked at him. 'Yes. Maybe it is.'

At once he saw Simon. Or rather his reflection, in the grimy garage window. Beyond the walls of the holiday cottage opposite, just sitting there. And waving, sadly.

Tom started to walk, fast. The girl walked with him. At the stile he stopped. 'I go across here.'

'Do you?' Interested, she looked over the field. 'You live in the back lane?'

'Martha's Cottage,' he said, without knowing why.

The girl seemed startled. 'Is it still called that? I used to live there.'

'You can't have.' Tom hefted the potatoes. 'We've always lived there.'

The girl laughed, amused, and walked away up the lane. 'Always,' she said drily. 'That's a very long time.'

SIXTEEN

'Where the hell were you?'

Tom scrambled furiously down the cliff-path, with Simon slithering behind. 'They were all in there!'

'I know . . .'

'I just felt so useless! I never know what to say. How to come up with something that'll make Tate think I'm more than some worm under his shoe.' Hot with humiliation he jumped down the last steps and pushed through the gorse. Its coconut smell rose around him, the branches whipping back, spiny and sharp.

Behind him, Simon muttered, 'You know how it is. I'd be there . . .'

Tom stopped and turned. 'Sometimes I think you just keep away for the hell of it.'

In the silence gulls cried. A flock of oystercatchers down on the tideline picked at the surf, making small runs and starts of movement.

'I'm not even alive,' Simon said drily. 'Remember?'

Slowly, Tom sank down on a rock. His throat felt dry and he was suddenly only too cold, the bleak wind off the sea cutting right through him. 'Of course you're alive,' he whispered. 'To me you are.'

'Not to anyone else.' Simon sat opposite. He had no coat on. He never needed one.

In the rock pool between their feet their twin reflections blurred and were scattered by rain. Tom reached out and grasped Simon's wrist. It was warm, the flesh firm. 'What does alive mean, anyway?' he muttered.

'Living.' Simon shrugged. 'Growing.'

'You do that. You're always the same age as me.'

'Maybe I am you. Have you ever thought that? The one you'd really like to be.'

Tom pulled his hand away. 'Don't be stupid.'

Simon shrugged. 'If you say so. Anyway, I'm here now, and so are you. Without your head punched in.'

Tom managed a weak smile. He stood up and wandered out on to the sands, hands in pockets, leaving footprints that filled with water in the wet, wobbly surface. 'If that girl hadn't come in it would have been worse.' He picked up a pebble and threw it, morosely. 'I hate them. All of them.'

'You're scared of them.'

Tom didn't bother to answer. They both knew he walked two miles over the cliff every morning and evening so as not to have to catch the school bus, that he spent lunch hours in the library or the gym with as many friends as he could find. 'School's hell,' he muttered.

Simon looked sly. 'It wouldn't be if you went to Darkwater Hall.'

Gulls flew up. Turning his head Tom saw someone walking along the tide, scavenging for driftwood. A big man, his hair cropped short, with an earring that glinted and an old, filthy coat tied with rope. A small black terrier ran barking into the waves.

'Who's he?'

Simon shrugged. 'Some traveller. He's got a fire up there.'

The man splashed up to them. He smelt of smoke and

sweat and beer. 'Well,' he said pleasantly. 'Tom. I've been waiting a long time to see thee.'

He had one eye missing. It made him look at you oddly.

Tom backed off. 'Sorry. I don't know you.'

'No laddie. Not yet.' The traveller hefted his bundle of wood and turned. 'But tha will.'

After a second Tom trailed after him. 'Are you . . . on the road?' The man wheezed with laughter. 'Aye. And a long road it is too. Long, and paved with good intentions.'

All across the beach he wheezed and coughed, the dog chasing waders joyously. As they came near the cliff Tom saw a small bright fire made up under an overhang, and a patched tent painted with clumsy sunflowers. Dumping the sticks, the man pulled out some cigarette papers, sat down, licked one, filled it and rolled it. Then he lit it and leaned back on a barnacled rock. 'I'm back. Make sure you tell her.'

'My mother?'

'No laddie! The girl. Have you seen her yet?'

Tom shook his head, bewildered. 'What girl?'

'I can't describe her. She'll be looking different these days. Just tell her the tramp's back and he's got a plan that'll keep her from Azrael's clutches. There's still time for us to do some 'at for her. What's the date, lad?'

'Twentieth of December.'

The traveller sucked his teeth. 'Eleven days left. We'll work it out, you tell her.' He held out the tin and papers to Tom, who shook his head, wondering if the man was some sort of mental case.

'Probably,' Simon whispered. 'Just our luck. Or maybe we could set him on Tate-face.'

Tom grinned. The traveller noticed. His one eye glanced slyly at Tom's left. ' 'Tis rude to whisper,' he murmured.

Tom stood, quickly. A shiver of danger went through him like a cold breeze. Simon was on his feet too.

'He can see me. I know he can.'

If he heard, the tramp took no notice. He puffed a small cloud of smoke out, his one good eye watching Tom's white face. 'Don't thee forget. Tell her she's done enough legwork for Azrael.'

'Azrael?'

'Aye.' The tramp scowled. 'Tha'll find out.'

'I've got to go.' Tom turned, climbing the cliff path hastily. He scrambled up the rocks, grabbing slippery handholds, feeling he was suddenly climbing away from nightmares, from Tate, the old man, even from Simon. For a moment he was alone and he was free, but as the drizzle closed in and he pushed into the wood towards the Hall, Simon came back and they walked silently together.

The short cut brought them out on the front drive. The tarmac had a small rainbow pool of oil where the taxi had waited. Signs in the parking bays said HEAD, DEPUTY, STAFF. Beds of flowers were frost-blackened and untidy, their brown stalks dead.

Above him, Darkwater Hall rose in gables and turrets. He went round to the back door and went in. The passage was flag-stoned and cold, so cold he didn't take his coat off but walked quickly down, leaving wet footprints on the stone.

He found his mother in the old Servants' Hall, now the canteen, pushing the big vacuum cleaner over the carpet. When she saw him she switched it off. The roar died abruptly.

'There you are! I thought you'd changed your mind. Get the shopping?'

He nodded.

His mother was a small, neat woman. Yesterday she'd had her hair cut for Christmas, a short bob. It made her look younger. She wound the flex up briskly. 'Don't look so crabby. I've asked Mr Scrab about you . . .'

'Who?'

She grinned. 'The relief caretaker. You'll love him, Tom. Anyway, go up to the Library.'

As he turned away she said 'Tom. I know it's not much of a way to spend your holiday.'

'It's OK.'

'No, it's not. But . . . money's tight. With Christmas coming. And you'll be a real help.'

He nodded, and went out.

The hall was silent, its noticeboards full of posters. He glanced at them. Football matches, rugby. Orchestra practice. Upstairs, rooms that might have once been for titled guests were lined with desks, huge blackboards nailed to the damask panels on the walls. Paintwork was dingy, carved here and there with names. Wooden floorboards creaked under him.

He took a mop and bucket from a cupboard, and in the room opposite saw ranks of expensive computers, silent under dustsheets. Going in he wandered among them, pausing at the window. Terraced gardens below were blurred by rain.

'You're right,' he muttered. 'I'd love to come here.'

Simon was pressing buttons on a keyboard. The screen

121

lit and he moved the text up absently. 'It'll never happen unless you ask.'

He knew that. And it was destroying him. For years now it had been his most secret dream, imagined lovingly at night before he slept, or in the worst lessons; the dream of being at Darkwater, where everyone would be intelligent and he would be someone. In the orchestra maybe. Certainly the rugby team. Watched by the girls. Effortlessly getting good results. Tall, handsome. Respected.

'You don't ask for much,' Simon said drily.

'I could do it. If I came here. And you don't have to pay, it's just passing an exam . . .'

'Then do it. What are you waiting for?'

'Mam wouldn't like it.'

Simon swivelled in the seat. 'You've never told her. I think you're scared you'll fail.'

Tom glared. Then he grabbed the mop, walked past him and straight up the stairs, where the rain pattered on the windows and the old paintings of forgotten people watched him in disdain.

The Library door was open. Someone was moving inside.

Tom went to the crack, and glanced in.

The long corridor was lined with books. Compared to this, the library at his school was a cupboard. But the books here always looked dusty and ancient, as if most of them were never looked at. Until now.

A man was leaning over a table, eagerly turning the pages of some vast volume from the back of a shelf; his fine hands smoothed the old sheets as if he loved them, as if they were precious to him.

Tom's foot creaked the floorboard. The man glanced up.

'Sorry.' Tom backed.

'Wait! Please!'

It was the man from the taxi. His hair was black, his narrow face lightly bearded. He wore dark casual clothes with an easy elegance, and as he came forward Tom saw he limped, as if he'd hurt himself.

'You're Tom? Is that right?'

Tom nodded.

The man looked slightly puzzled. 'Is there just you?'

'Yes.'

'I see. Well, earlier, I spoke with your mother. She said you'd be kind enough to give me a hand with my equipment.' He smiled, a shy smile, and to Tom's surprise a small black cat jumped up onto the books and rubbed against him. The man picked the cat up and stroked its ears.

'I'm the new chemistry teacher,' he said quietly. 'My name is Azrael.'

SEVENTEEN

'Put that stuff away. You won't need it.' Azrael came and took the mop and bucket gently from him, and dumped them behind a door.

'I thought you wanted . . .'

'Not that sort of work.' The man stood back and looked at him, an almost troubled look. 'This is a strange place for a boy of your age, Tom. You should be out with the village boys. Or at least, doing some schoolwork.'

Tom went red.

The cat mewed.

'Oh, I'm sorry,' Azrael said at once. 'Stupid thing to say.' He seemed embarrassed, turning and putting the book back on its shelf. 'I have a terrible habit of interfering; please forget I said it.'

'It doesn't matter.'

'Yes . . . well look, I have to set up my laboratory. I've made a start, but I really need an assistant. It's down here.'

He turned and walked quickly down the corridor of books, the cat stalking after him, its tail high.

'A real nutcase,' Simon whispered.

Tom ignored him. Azrael's remark had stung him. It was right. What on earth was he doing here, scrubbing floors? He should be studying, reading, doing everything he could to get the highest grades, to get away from the stupid hateful Tates. Why did he waste so much of his time?

They came to the doors of the room at the end; a room which was always kept locked, as far as Tom knew. But the dark man took a bunch of keys from his pocket and fitted one carefully into the lock.

'I do hope Scrab's brought everything,' he said thoughtfully.

'Well yer needn't get yerself in a twist about that.' The testy voice came from behind; Tom turned in alarm.

'All yer junk's in there. And there's this great ugly contraption. Gawd knows what yer want with it all.'

A small, round-shouldered man in a grubby white overall was shuffling sideways down the passage. He carried a large domed jar, and his greasy hair was slicked back, leaving a scatter of dandruff on the dusty glass he struggled with. He lowered it wearily to the floor and glared at Tom.

'This the new one?'

'That's right,' Azrael said quietly.

'Only 'im? I thought there was—'

'Tom,' Azrael said instantly. 'Would you mind carrying the jar in for Mr Scrab? I think he finds it heavy.' He gave a covert glare at the little man and turned, and Scrab shrugged carelessly at his back. 'Suit yerself. Just don't get ringing down for coffee and fancy cakes in this lifetime. Yer'll get none.'

The jar was heavy. As Tom lifted it Azrael said, 'Oh, I think I might.' He turned the key. Then he flung the two doors wide.

The Laboratory was astonishing. On the walls great murals were painted, of constellations and Zodiac symbols – a huge crab, a water-carrier, a scorpion scattering golden stars from its tail. A telescope stood at one window, brand new. From crates and boxes straw spilled out, and Tom saw the edges of flasks and test tubes, scales and burners. An electron microscope stood on the bench. In one corner a computer screen flickered. And from the ceiling, an ancient mechanical model of the planets drifted silently in the sudden draught.

Azrael looked pleased. 'This is excellent. Here the Great Work can really go on.'

He went in. Scrab scratched thin hair and stared gloomily at Tom. 'Go on,' he said. 'Enjoy yerself.' Then he turned and shuffled down the corridor.

Tom staggered in and lowered the jar carefully onto a bench.

'Who is HE?'

'The caretaker.' Azrael was pulling complicated zigzags of glass out of a packing case. 'Essentially harmless.'

'He seems to know you.'

'We've worked together before.' Azrael glanced over. 'Set this up first. All right?'

'Whatever you say.'

It was better than scrubbing floors. All afternoon he assembled a vast mass of tubing, piecing it together from Azrael's absent-minded instructions; parts for distillation, filters, tripods. He unrolled diagrams and charts and pinned them up, and a huge Periodic Table with the names of the elements in strange text like a spell – Iridium, Rhodium, Helium. There were boxes of labelled specimens that had to be arranged on shelves, and other things that he thought bizarre for a chemistry lab – a drawing of the human body, a statue of Anubis, small copper bells, a feathered dream-catcher. All the while

Azrael unpacked notebooks and papers, rifling through them with muttered comments.

At last Tom looked round. 'Is all this yours?'

'Just a few bits and pieces.'

'Doesn't the school have stuff?' He tugged open a crate and saw rows of gleaming crucibles. 'Some of this looks pretty old-fashioned. I don't do chemistry, but is this the right sort of thing?'

Azrael smiled briefly. 'Let's say I have my own ways. What are your subjects, Tom?'

'History, English, Maths.'

'Maths! Good. That will be useful.'

Behind him, Simon examined the telescope. 'Not just a nutcase,' he muttered. 'But a rich one.'

Outside, the short December day died quickly, the sun setting in a brief red hollow in the clouds. Finally, Azrael glanced up. Fiery light caught the edge of his face. 'Right. That's enough for now. And despite Scrab's mutterings, I'm thirsty, aren't you?'

He went to the fireplace and pressed an old buttonpush there. 'None of those work,' Tom said. 'Otherwise all the kids would be pressing them.'

Azrael shrugged gracefully. 'You never know.'

He cleared a space on a bench, pulled up two chairs and sat on one, resting his feet on the other with a sigh.

'So. This is a nice place. Do you enjoy living here, Tom?'

'It's OK.'

'Sea. Beaches. The moor. Lots of wealthy visitors. Quite idyllic.'

'It could be,' Tom said shortly. He played with the computer flex. Azrael watched him closely. Then the doorhandle turned. Azrael sat up delighted. 'What did I tell you?'

Scrab must have been expecting the call. He came in with two mugs of tea on a tray and a chipped plate of shortbread biscuits, which he dumped on the papers with bad grace.

'As if I 'ad nowt better to do.'

'Your reward will come,' Azrael said coolly, 'in the next world.'

'Aye. And yer so sharp yer'll cut yerself.' The cat on the chair by the radiator stopped licking itself and stared at him.

'Any sign?' Azrael asked quietly.

'Not yet. Got till New Year, ain't she?'

'Indeed.'

'What if she don't show? If we 'as to go looking?'

'She can never go far enough.' Azrael poured the tea thoughtfully. 'Not in all the twelve dimensions. Not from me.'

Tom listened. Simon was wandering between the benches; he came to the glass jar and gazed in, his face distorted in the thick, bubbled sides.

'Well,' Scrab said, sliding out. 'She did all right with 'er time. One of yer better bargains.'

Azrael gave a sharp sideways nod at the door. Scrab spat in the empty fireplace, and went.

'Tell me,' Azrael leaned forward. 'Do you have any brothers or sisters, Tom?'

The suddenness of the question threw him. 'One.' Then, instantly, 'None.'

'A bit confusing.' Azrael selected a biscuit daintily.

Tom shrugged. 'I was one of twins. The other one –

my brother – died. At least, he wasn't born properly.'

Azrael's hand was still. Then he dropped the biscuit back on the plate. 'I see.' His voice was strange. He got up and wandered to the jar, holding it with both hands, looking in, as Simon had done. 'That explains things. It must have been hard on your parents.'

Tom sipped uneasily at the tea. 'I suppose.'

'And you.'

'I was just a baby.'

Azrael turned. The room was very dark now; he leaned over and plugged a lamp in, and the sudden glow woke reflections in hundreds of glass surfaces, and in the eyes of the Anubis statue. 'And you go to this school?'

'No.' Tom stood, putting the mug down. 'Look, I should be going.'

'No? But it would be so suitable!' Azrael's hands spread wide on the jar. He turned. 'Wouldn't it? Wouldn't you like to come here?'

Tom was at the door. 'Yes,' he breathed 'but . . .'

Azrael took a step forward. To Tom's surprise he pulled what seemed to be a playing card out of a pocket and laid it on the bench and looked at it. It was the Jack of Clubs. 'But what?'

'I don't know.' Tom's voice was tight; he felt as if he couldn't breathe. 'I've got to go.'

'Look.' Azrael came up to him. 'I need help with my work. I have vital research going on.' He smiled, coyly. 'You'd enjoy it, and you'd learn a lot. Five pounds an hour, when you can come. Is that fair?'

He was amazed and oddly relieved. 'More than fair.'

'Excellent. Up to Christmas and after. Until . . . oh let's say until New Year, shall we?'

Downstairs, the Hall was in darkness. Paula had gone; her overall swung on its hook. Tom let himself out into the cold. Overhead the frosty stars glinted; far out to sea a great cloudbank streamed from the west. As he stood in the porch the gargoyles were openmouthed against the light. Behind, footsteps stirred the crisp leaves.

'I wondered where you'd got to,' he said. 'Did you hear what he's paying?'

There was no answer. He turned, quickly. 'Simon?'

Cloud drifted from the moon; eerie light lit the eyes of the gargoyles, their gleaming teeth.

Under them, the blonde girl from the Post Office was watching him curiously.

EIGHTEEN

He stared at her. 'Where did you spring from?'

'Keep your voice down!' She glanced at the moon, anxiously; cloud was drifting over it again. 'Is Azrael in there?'

'Yes. But . . .'

'Blast.' She swung the rucksack up; it seemed heavy. He remembered the tins of food she had bought. 'One of those thugs in the Post Office said your mother was the cleaner here.'

He was annoyed. 'So?'

'So you owe me a favour. I need you to get me inside. And I need a key. Someone's changed all the locks.'

'I can't!'

'Of course you can.'

Tom was silent. There was something about her that puzzled him. Something not quite right. Over his shoulder he said to Simon, 'What is it?'

'Never mind him,' the girl snapped. 'Give me the key.'

Astonished, they stared at her.

'You can see me?' Simon came out of the shadows, intensely interested. 'You really can?'

'Why shouldn't I?'

'This is brilliant!'

'Quiet!' Tom shook his head. This scared him. 'If it's thieving, forget it.'

The girl looked tired. She almost smiled. 'I just need

131

somewhere to stay. Till New Year. This place is empty till term. There are plenty of beds.'

An owl hooted; she looked out anxiously. 'You owe me. No one else need know, not your mother. Especially not Azrael.'

'And Mr Scrab?'

She sighed. 'Him too.'

A window clattered above them. Instantly the three of them flattened into the shadows, Tom feeling Simon's warmth at his shoulder. A slot of faint light shone out briefly into the dark trees, a man's indistinct shadow flitting across it. Then the shutters were slammed.

The girl hissed with relief. 'Let's get inside.'

'But he's living here. Azrael. Isn't it . . .'

'It doesn't matter where I go in the end. Now come on!'

Tom hesitated. 'Do it,' Simon said quickly.

So he unlocked the door, turning the well-oiled catch silently. As they slipped in he whispered, 'I don't know your name.'

'Sarah.' She looked round the black and white hall.

Tom bit his lip 'You could go . . .'

'I know where to go,' she muttered. Quickly she climbed the curved stairs and they followed, among small creaks of floorboards and the old building's shifts and murmurs in the windy night. The girl knew the way. She went up to the old servants' quarters, tiptoeing carefully past the Library wing. Everything was in darkness. Azrael must have gone to bed, Tom thought.

The servants' stair was a mass of shadows; they inched their way up, keeping to the edge of the steps, Sarah letting a small mouse run over her feet with only a sudden intake of breath.

Beyond the alcove filled with filing cabinets she seemed suddenly lost. 'They've changed this,' she whispered, close to his ear. 'There used to be a corridor here.'

'Through there.' He opened the fire door; it slid behind them with a slow swish. This area was the sixth-form bedrooms; in his wanderings he'd been up here often, pretending, dreaming. He had a favourite room half way down that he used as his. To his surprise, that was the door she stopped at.

'My room. Open it.'

He fumbled with the keys. Around them the vast house was silent, the only sound the chink of iron in the lock and almost too far off to hear, the thunder of the tide in Newhaven Bay.

And suddenly, something else.

A low sound. It rose from the depths of the house, so that Simon muttered 'Listen,' and the key stopped in mid-turn.

Water. Deep, rumbling water, as if it ran inside them, in their veins, vibrating, a sound almost felt.

The girl was the first to move. 'The Darkwater. Haven't you heard it before?'

'Sometimes. It's not often you can.'

'Give me that.' She took the keys, slid off the ones she needed, and dumped the rest back in his hands. 'You'll get them back.'

Then she had opened the door and slipped through. He took a step after her; the wooden panels closed firmly in his face.

'See you tomorrow,' the keyhole whispered.

In the morning he took the long way round the village. Up Deerham Lane and over the fields. It was cold and the sky was grey, and Simon ran ahead and opened the small kissing-gates for him so he wouldn't have to take his hands out of his pockets.

'It sounds a nice job,' his mother had said last night, eating toast and turning the newspaper pages. 'I'm amazed he's paying you so much.'

So was Tom. 'What about this girl?' he asked now.

'On the run,' Simon said wisely. 'You watch the papers, there'll be something.'

'Should we tell someone?'

His brother shrugged, climbed the last stile and jumped down. 'Not till we know more. One thing; she's been in that school before.'

'Ex-pupil?'

'Too young.'

'Maybe she came and then left.'

'Possible.'

Tom climbed the stile and walked into the wood. 'Her face is familiar,' he said softly.

At the Devil's Quoits someone had broken the iron fence around the stones. On the largest one was written STEVE WAS HERE in white letters made from straggly dollops of paint. Standing looking at it, hands in pockets, was Azrael.

He glanced up darkly. 'Look at this! Who's Steve?'

Tom shrugged. 'Probably Tate. His father runs the Post Office.' Then, hastily, he added, 'But don't say I said so.'

Azrael glanced at him sidelong. 'Don't get on?'

'No.'

Azrael laughed. He had his dark coat on. 'I'm just taking a stroll round the old place Tom. I'd be grateful if you'd go up to the Lab and start up. I've left instructions. Be careful of the one burner; it takes ages to light.'

He turned. Tom said 'What sort of research is it?'

Azrael ducked under the low fir branches. 'Didn't I say? Transmutation. Of elements. A very long process.'

There was no sign of Scrab, and Paula had gone to Truro Christmas shopping, so he went up and tapped on the girl's door. 'Sarah? It's Tom.'

No answer.

He tried the handle, but it was locked. Worried, he wandered down to the Library, where Simon was waiting.

'Maybe she's gone.'

'No such luck,' Tom said gloomily.

Azrael's instructions were written on a rectangular white card pinned to the mantelshelf. Tom assembled the listed glassware, spooning in chemicals from the rows of jars over the shelf. The bottles of acid were huge and heavy; he poured from them with infinite care, seeing one drop of the sulphuric escape and burn into the bench with a whiff of acrid vapour.

The room filled with dim, unpleasant smells.

Simon lit the burner, turning it up so the flame roared whitehot, and Tom scowled at him. 'Stop messing.'

'Your trouble,' Simon sighed, 'is that you're too serious. That's why they make fun of you.'

His brother jammed the stopper in furiously. 'Drop dead.'

Simon giggled, and went over to the wall safe. 'I wonder what's in here.'

'It's locked. And Azrael keeps the key.'

The girl was leaning inside the door; she came in and closed it and looked round. 'Well. This brings it all back.'

Tom straightened. 'I think you should tell us . . . I mean . . . We don't know anything about you.'

Amused, she perched on a bench, her feet on a stool. She wore muddy walking boots and a thick fleece jacket, expensive-looking. Her hair was dyed. She looked about sixteen, he thought.

'Tell you what?'

'Well, have you run off?'

'No.'

'Left home, I mean.'

'No.' She grinned. 'The opposite. This is my home.'

'It's a school.' Simon said, and came and sat by the telescope. She looked at him. 'Maybe it is, now. But not always. I used to live here; in fact I still own the place. I'm Sarah Trevelyan.'

Tom turned the burner down; the hot hissing died but the heat had warmed the lab. 'Her descendant, you mean? Sarah Trevelyan was the woman who made this place a school – they read her will every year on Founder's Day. A kid that goes here told me. She left money so that . . .'

'Every child that is able, whether boy or girl, rich or poor, may receive, without payment, the education that their heart desires. I know. I wrote it.'

A flask bubbled, suddenly. Tom stared at her. 'Are you crazy?'

Sarah smiled, sadly. She hugged her knees. 'I've dreaded

this, but now it's come, it's such a relief. Keeping a secret for a hundred years is a torment – it bubbles inside you like that potion – it's never still and you can't stop it rising to the surface.' She laughed at their bemused look. The shapes of the planets began to drift in the warming air.

'I was born in 1885. I made an arrangement with a . . . creature. A supernatural power. The one you know as Azrael. He gave me a hundred years to live, and my own estate and fortune. The time runs out at New Year. That's why he's come back. He's come for me.'

'Oh yes,' Tom said. 'And I'm the Queen of Sheba.'

Sarah shrugged. 'Kids. I thought you'd be different.' She glanced at Simon. 'Having him around, I mean.'

'What about him.'

She got up, impatient. 'All right. I'll prove it. Come on.'

She went to the door and out along the crowded library corridor with its chained volumes to a room by the entrance to the wing. On one wall a mothy rhinoceros head peered down. On the other was a painting.

Tom had seen it many times. The young Sarah Trevelyan looked down at him from a luxurious Victorian sofa. Her dress was dark blue, with an ivory lace collar, her brown hair long and intricately pinned.

'It looks like you,' Simon said, considering. 'Was she your great-grandmother?'

'It's me.' Sarah stood with her back to the painting.

The likeness was incredible, if you could ignore the short blonde hair. Tom was shaken, but he shrugged.

'How could it . . .'

'Look at her hands.'

The girl in the painting had her hands on her lap. She was looking at the watcher with an amused, knowing smile, and her palms were turned up. Across one of them were five red weals.

Sarah held up her own hand, facing him.

Five red marks crossed it. Identical.

'I had it painted like that deliberately, though the wretched artist had to be nagged to put them in. I knew I might need them.' She leaned back against the bookshelves. Tom said, carefully, 'How did you get them?'

'Beaten. You think they should have faded in a hundred years, don't you? But when the clocks started ticking, I just stopped. My nails didn't grow, my hair stayed the same length. I never lost a tooth or an eyelash. It took me a while to notice it, but then I knew I was static. The world moved around me, but I never grew up.'

She smiled, spinning an old Empire globe, fingering the dusty countries absently. 'It's so ironic. I never wanted to grow old. What I did want was knowledge, and I got it. Do you know how many schools I've been to? At least sixteen, till I got sick of it. I've got dozens of exams – O Levels, A levels, Certificates, even a few GCSEs. I've had jobs – in the wars it was easy; I worked on the land, in factories, got evacuated from London. I've travelled too. Rome, Paris, I know them like you know that beach down there. Every country in Europe, I trailed round them, learned their languages, saw their history happen, was in Berlin when the Wall came down. Trouble was, it wasn't the sort of knowledge I really wanted. Maybe it took me the first fifty years to realise that.'

They were staring at her. She looked away, up at the

picture. How could she tell them how it had all been, that hundred years? More than a lifetime, places and people she could barely remember, all the friends, enemies, houses, mistakes, brief happinesses. And it had changed her. Azrael had known it would.

She remembered the moment the clocks had started; that was vivid, even after all this time. And it was still here, the one on the mantelshelf, still ticking, as it had ticked all down the years. 'That first day I told myself Azrael was mad,' she said. 'That he'd just gone home, to wherever he came from. But when the days passed, and months, and I didn't age, then I knew, I really knew I had done it. I had sold my soul.'

Tom leaned against the window and folded his arms. If she was lying she was good at it. 'People would find out,' he said.

'They almost did, a few times. My father died six years after we came back here, and I lived here two more years, but I knew by then I dare not stay anywhere too long. So Sarah Trevelyan endowed her school and went to live abroad, and after that I did everything through letters to the solicitors. When I wrote the will I left the money to myself – my own daughter. And so on. But I couldn't make friends my own age, because there were none. I'm still sixteen! And yet I'm not.' She smiled, going over to the telescope. 'I used to be pretty selfish. I thought having money was important. Then I felt sorry for the villagers – we used to call them the poor, and my God, they were. I tried to help them, to undo what the Trevelyans had done.'

'That was good,' Tom said at random.

She turned, sharply. 'Yes. But it took me too long to

139

find out that the poor had more than me. Family, for one thing. A hundred years is a lot of loneliness.'

Tom bit his lip. 'But Azrael. Does that mean he's as old as . . .'

'Older. He comes from the world's beginning, that one. Are you working for him?'

'Yes. He's paying . . .'

'Oh he pays well, but don't make any deals. And never—'

Footsteps came up the stairs. Sarah turned quickly. 'He's back. I don't want to see him. Not yet. I've still got ten days left.'

'But won't he know?'

'I don't care!' She backed into the maze of rooms. The Library door opened. Azrael's voice said 'It's me, Tom.'

Sarah glanced round. 'The fire escape.'

They raced through the rooms of books and papers. 'Look at it,' she muttered. 'As much a mess as ever.'

Simon had the fire door open.

'Tom?' Azrael called.

Pages ruffled in the chill breeze. Sarah climbed out and crouched.

'Never what?' Tom hissed.

She grabbed the collar of his coat. 'Never touch the jar. The big one, the one in the safe.'

And then, just as he shut the door, she whispered, 'Because I think I may be the one who killed your brother.'

NINETEEN

Christmas was almost here.

Tom's mother got the box of decorations down from the attic and he had to put them up, pushing the drawing pins into last year's holes. Paula always enjoyed Christmas. She made the small cottage cosy, burning logs on the hearth and making swathes of ivy and holly across the fireplace. Lamps were lit and the best china came out, and extravagant cheap boxes of chocolates from Truro market. The house smelt of brandy and fruit cake.

That evening Steve Tate's dad dropped the tree off in his van. Tom kept well out of the way. From the upstairs window he saw Steve in the passenger seat with his feet on the dashboard, whistling to the loud thump of music. He turned his head and glanced up.

Tom dropped the curtain and jumped back. Just too late.

'Where's your girlfriend, lover boy?' Steve shouted. He took something small out of his pocket and held it up. 'Be seeing you,' he grinned.

Tom stood still, chilled and puzzled. It had looked like a key.

All evening his mother decorated the tree with tinsel and small wooden angels painted gold, their tiny haloes needing straightening after months in the box. They'd had them for years. When he'd been small Tom's favourite had been the one with the tiny broken foot; he picked it off the floor now and handed it up to her. As she hung it he went back to wrapping the presents while Simon lounged on the sofa and ate crisps.

What had Sarah meant? How could she have killed Simon? It didn't make any sense, and it scared him. Like this crazy story of a hundred years of life. Had she deliberately cut her hands to match that portrait?

Folding the silver paper with its galloping reindeer he bit the tape off and looked at Simon, who muttered, 'Just imagine for one minute it's true. Think of all the things she's lived through! Both World Wars. The sixties. Politics, fashions, inventions.'

'Maybe.' He turned the parcel over.

His mother put the last star on the treetop, and flicked the switch. Red and blue and gold, small lights sparked into brilliance, lighting the green secret spaces of the tree. Hands on hips she looked at the room with satisfaction.

'That's more like it.'

That night in bed, he was cold. Frost was forming outside the window, a white intricate pattern. Deep under the bedclothes he muttered, 'So what happens to her on New Year's Eve?'

'He takes her away. To some dark, supernatural place.'

Tom was silent. Then he said, 'She's scared. And what does that make Azrael?'

Simon sighed sleepily and turned over. 'God knows. Ask Sarah.'

He couldn't. There was no sign of her. Next day, the twenty-third, he went up and hammered on the bedroom door twice but there was no answer, and it was firmly locked. But when he came down to the Lab and put on the white coat Azrael had lent him, his fingers touched something icy in the pocket and he pulled out the keys he had given her; one for the upstairs room and one for the outside door. So had she gone? Or had copies made? That worried him. Things might go missing. It would be his fault.

Azrael said, 'Stop day-dreaming, Tom.'

'Sorry.' He dropped the keys back and glanced quickly at the watch; an old-fashioned fob watch. He was timing a peculiar process; Azrael was dripping a liquid from a pipette into a flask, one drop every two minutes. Exactly.

'Now,' Tom said.

The globule grew, wobbled, fell. It spread on the pink stuff in the flask, giving off a brief stink.

'Mmm,' Azrael muttered.

'This afternoon,' Tom said, 'I have to help out downstairs. Getting things ready for the Waits.'

'The Waits?'

'A sort of Carol Service. By candlelight. It starts off in the great hall every Christmas Eve. The Founder gave money for it.'

'Ah.' Azrael smiled narrowly. 'The Founder.'

Tom glanced at him. 'You must know about her,' he said carefully. 'Oh . . . now.'

Azrael squeezed the pipette delicately. Another drop fell. 'Suppose you tell me,' he said slyly.

'Be careful,' Simon muttered.

Tom ignored him. 'Her name was Sarah Trevelyan. She started this school. She made it so that local people – poor people – could have an education without needing any money. Fishermen's sons, and girls from the factories.'

'How very generous.' Azrael stirred the mixture

smoothly. 'And what else did she do?'

Tom kept his eyes on the watch. Maybe she'd been lying after all. 'Plenty. There are the Trevelyan almshouses, the village library, the old people's cottages down Gannet Lane. She paid for the harbour defences and the lifeboat. There's a Trevelyan Scholarship for something, and all sorts of charities and funds. Now.'

The drop plipped.

'You forgot the Cottage Hospital,' Azrael said mildly.

Tom's heart thumped. He looked up, and a gull screamed by the window. 'If you knew, why ask?'

Azrael shrugged. 'I suppose I like to hear it. So many good things in one lifetime. Why do you suppose she spent all that money on her tenants, Tom? She must have been an extraordinary woman.'

The door creaked. Scrab's greasy head came round it.

'Staying for Christmas are yer?'

Azrael gave a delicate smile. 'I'll be away. Just for the day.'

'Ah. Knew it.'

He withdrew, tripped over the cat, and swore.

'Now!' said Tom, remembering.

The pink liquid heaved. It separated. Faint coils of smoke rose from it.

'Have you seen her?' Azrael asked quietly.

In the utter silence the rasp of the cat's tongue was enormous. A sudden hiss of sleet rattled the windows. Tom looked up.

'Yes,' he said.

'I suspected as much. Mephisto said the room held the scent of her yesterday. So she's early. And the father of lies, the tramp, is back too.'

Tom dumped the watch on the bench and whirled round to face him.

'Who are you?' he breathed.

Azrael smiled sadly. 'That would take too long to explain.'

'What do you want with her! She's scared!'

'She has no need.'

'She said you'd come for her.'

'That much, I'm afraid, is true. She has,' Azrael glanced at the almanac on the wall, 'eight days left.'

'Then what?'

'The price must be paid.'

'What price? Her life?'

'Time, Tom?'

'What?'

'TIME!' Azrael glanced at him in sudden anxiety. 'When? WHEN?'

'I don't know!' Tom grabbed for the watch. 'Now! No! Wait!'

But the drop wobbled and fell, and the flask erupted into an instant acrid yellow hissing steam that made them cough, clouds of it mushrooming up and filling the room, so that the cat spat and ran, and Azrael had to rush over and wrench the window open, and they both hung out coughing and retching.

Cold sleet slashed their faces. In the bitter gale the sea to its horizon was empty, a spumy-grey agitation of waves, the clifftops sheep-gnawed and deserted.

Azrael turned, leaning his back against the sill. He took out a silk handkerchief and glanced ruefully at Tom.

'Sorry,' Tom gasped.

The dark man was still a moment, wiping his eyes.

Then he sighed gracefully, and limped back to the scorched and ruined flask.

'Still a few more things to add,' he said quietly.

'I should have remembered to tell her about the tramp!'

'She might know by now.' Simon opened the gate to the Bear Garden and listened. 'Voices.'

'Tate?' Tom said instantly.

'Don't be paranoid.'

In the twilit garden the bears were dark blue shadows, glinting with frost. From the claws of one a great icicle hung. Tom listened. There was the far-off sea, and a fox up on the moor. There was a car on the road. And there were two voices.

They were coming from a small summerhouse that leaned in one corner, its dilapidated roof mended with corrugated iron. Old cricket stumps and a lawnmower were stored in it. Now light gleamed from its cracks.

Simon crept nearer, Tom close behind. The grass was crisp under him, the shadow of the Hall blackening the lawns.

'It's her,' Simon whispered. He moved aside, and Tom saw Sarah. She had her back to him.

'When?' a voice asked her.

'Tomorrow night. Or better still, Christmas Day. That's a good time for it.'

'No chance. For a start he won't stay here, girlie.' They recognized the tramp's wheeze. 'Too holy a night for the likes of him.'

Tom stepped closer.

Instantly a dog gave a short yelping bark. Through the door's crack he saw Sarah turn.

'Is it the hounds?' the tramp breathed.

'No.' Sarah opened the door and pulled Tom in. 'It's your useless messengers.'

The summerhouse was lit by a single candle stuck in a splintered table. The tramp had been lounging in an old striped deckchair; now he sank back in relief. 'Lord, laddies. I thought it was all up with us then.'

Tom looked at Sarah. 'Azrael will be away for Christmas. And he knows you're here.'

She shrugged, sitting on an upturned bucket.

'She thinks,' the tramp said in disgust, 'that talking to him will help. Asking him, all polite like, to let her be. Useless folly. No one gets clear of that one.'

Sarah glared at him. 'This is my problem.'

'And I'm sent, girlie, to help thee solve it. Of course, if tha'd listened to me before . . .'

She stood, scowling. 'Forget it. My mind's made up. And I've got things to do. A new will to write, for a start.' She glared at Tom. 'You stay out of this. I've had a hundred years to get used to the idea.'

'Aye.' The tramp took out his cigarettes, 'And how thou'll pay for 'em.'

Sarah marched to the door. 'Get out of my way,' she snapped, and as Simon moved she swept past him into the dark night.

The tramp rolled a cigarette. 'Trevelyan to the core,' he said, with a sort of pride. 'She won't beg, whatever she thinks. 'Tis we that'll have to do it then.'

'Do what?'

'What she won't. Azrael wants a soul. That's his right. But he's fond of a bargain. All we have to do is get him a substitute.'

He puffed. Blue smoke drifted. 'Who's thy worst enemy in all the world, Tom?'

'Steve Tate,' Tom said, without hesitation.

The tramp winked, shook the match out and threw it away. 'And how would thou like to be rid of him for ever, eh?'

TWENTY

The darkness was crooked.

It was wet, the earth a sludge sliding under him, and then the stench making him feel sick, a stench of rottenness, of stems and stalks crushed, and the bloated, lightstarved polyps of fungi that grew on the softening pit-props.

His leg hurt. He drifted in and out of the darkness, but always the pain troubled him and the rain woke him by dripping on his face. Simon was there, and it wasn't soft earth his head was propped on but Simon's lap, and it was Simon who was yelling desperately to the searchers above. But no one could hear him.

Tom shifted, and deep under his ear in hollow caves an invisible river roared. 'Hello lover boy,' it thundered. 'See you tomorrow.'

He woke, instantly.

'What's wrong?' Simon muttered.

A farm lorry grumbled by outside. Early lights were on in the houses towards the harbour. A robin was singing. It was Christmas Eve.

Slowly, Tom let himself relax.

'I was dreaming about being down that pit. I'd have died if it hadn't been for you.'

'Too right.' Simon lay with his arms behind his head. 'Kept you warm, kept you alive. Don't think I've ever talked so much in my . . . life.'

Tom almost smiled, lying back on the pillow. He had been nearly three days in the bottom of the shaft. When they had pulled him up on the swinging stretcher he had seen all their faces looking down at him, circling crazily, and his mother's had been white and creased, as if the long terror had dried everything up in her, shrivelled her life. And he had never told anyone Steve Tate had pushed him in.

But now he said, 'I told the tramp to get lost. It's a mad idea.'

'But tempting.' Simon considered. 'I mean, really tempting. Look at Tate, the scum of the earth. Think how he's likely to turn out. Then look at Sarah. All the things she's done. Who most deserves to live? It's no contest.'

'I don't want him dead.' Tom drew his knees up and clasped them.

'Don't you?'

'No. Not dead. Just . . .'

'In Hell,' Simon whispered.

He was quiet at breakfast.

'Going up to the Hall?' Paula asked, putting lipstick on. 'Or has the mad scientist given you the day off?'

'Sort of. He's not mad. He's OK.'

Paula pursed her lips. 'I tell you what, he's handsome. Is he married?'

He looked at her in alarm and she giggled. He liked it when she did that.

He spent most of the day lazing around, avoiding the Hall. He and Simon walked the cliffpath along to Mamble and back, and all the way they saw no one, only

150

skuas and terns and the grey round heads of seals out in the choppy waters. It rained once, a great lowering shower that pattered against Tom's hood, and when they got back home the tree was lit in the window and the house seemed a refuge.

Simon, quite dry, sat on the windowseat and said, 'We should invite Sarah over for Christmas dinner. She'll be all on her own up there. A few tins of beans isn't much to live on.'

Tom pulled on a dry sock. 'We could.' He knew his mother would tease him, though.

As it got dark he stood at the window and watched the twilight gather. Another day lost. There were only seven left now. The worry of it mingled oddly inside him with the secret excitement of Christmas. As if something huge would happen.

They had a lift up to the Hall from John Hubbard, who ran the local taxi. Tom sat in the back with Simon, and as they turned into the drive he saw to his surprise that it was lit all along its length with white lanterns, each burning a strange blueish flame.

'These are new!'

Paula nodded. 'Scrab put them up. I don't know where he got them.'

The driveway was thronged with people. And Darkwater Hall was alive, its door wide open, all its windows lit. Great swags of holly hung down the bannisters and in the black and white hall an enormous tree stood, extravagantly decorated with tartan bows and candles.

Tom took a mince pie off a tray, and a glass of hot wine.

'Not too much of that stuff,' his mother muttered, but two of her friends came over then and he managed to slip away. Behind him, at the foot of the stairs, the band started up with 'The First Nowell', and the Waits got themselves together in a chattering, fussy straggle.

The Waits were the singers, of all ages; lots of children, men with lanterns, women well wrapped up with scarves and hip-flasks. They whistled and clapped as the Grey Mare came prancing out, the skeleton of a horse's head decked with ribbons and mounted on a stick; a sheet was pinned round it and the horse's jaw clacked as the man underneath pulled the strings. They would carry it round the parish; an eerie, half-forgotten custom. It had always scared him stiff when he was a kid.

'Enjoying yourself?'

Sarah was standing behind him, nibbling a mince pie. She looked tired and strained, her hair lank and unwashed. In the crowd no one had noticed her. He stepped back. 'Are you?'

'Yes.' She glanced round, defiantly. 'It's nice to see the things I started are still going strong.'

'Don't pretend. You must be worried.'

'And the Mare too!' She licked her fingers. 'I got really interested in folklore. Well, for the first thirty years.'

'Sarah. There must be . . .'

'I told you.' She turned, angry. 'You don't need to feel sorry for me! Besides, I'm going to talk to Azrael. Where is he?'

The carol rose to its chorus. Tom shrugged, unhappily. 'In the Lab?'

'Right.' She turned; he drank the last of the wine in a gulp and followed, pushing through the crowd to the stairs, dumping the plate and glass and running up after her, the hot drink pulsing in his head. Below them the carol ended with clapping; the band swung into the slow solemnity of 'Silent Night'.

But Azrael wasn't in the Lab. As they came to the door on the first floor with HEADMASTER on it they saw the cat. It was washing on the woven matting. It looked up at them.

'I should have known,' Sarah said drily. She turned the handle.

It was a huge room, and a fire was burning in the hearth. Azrael was standing with his back to them by the tall windows, looking out into the night. He wore his long outdoor coat, as if he was waiting for some taxi. Perhaps he saw their reflections. He was smiling when he turned.

'My dear Sarah! After all this time.'

'Hello Azrael. You haven't altered a bit.' She walked across the soft carpet to a small table covered with a cloth, then sat down and poured some tea, calmly.

For years she had dreaded this moment. Yet now it had come it was nothing but relief. It had been a fierce defiance that had brought her back; if she had to die, here was as good as anywhere, it was hers at least, the place she had sold her soul for. And she had forgotten how likeable Azrael always was.

'Two cups,' she said quietly. 'You were expecting me.'

Azrael tipped his head. 'Of course. I have been for some days.'

She spooned in sugar. 'I did think about staying away. Hiding out in South America or somewhere. I could still go.'

'Nowhere would be far enough, Sarah.'

She glanced at Tom. 'Sit down. And where's your brother?'

Tom shrugged, surprised. He realised he hadn't seen Simon since they arrived. Azrael's eyes watched him, strangely bright.

'Two things. That's all I want,' Sarah said quickly, watching Tom sit. 'First of all, was I responsible for Simon's death? I need to know that.'

Azrael looked shocked, then concerned. He came over to the sofa.

'You?'

'I saw you both.' She turned to Tom. 'Long before you were born, in a sort of . . . jar he has. I dropped it, well almost. You were all shaken up. I need to know!' she snapped at Azrael. 'Whether what happened to them later was because of that.'

Azrael frowned and sat, slowly. Finally he said, 'I had no idea this was on your mind. The truth is, Sarah, I don't know. All things are connected in the Great Work, all times and places, all minds. Everything that has ever happened in the world is threaded with everything else in a vast intricate web. Whether things would have worked out differently is not for us to know. You meant no harm. You were only curious.' He glanced over. 'I'm sure Tom doesn't blame you.'

'Of course I don't!' Tom felt hot. He had never heard anything so ridiculous.

'All right.' Sarah nodded, nettled. 'So you won't tell me.'

'I can't, believe me. I have no knowledge of . . .'

'Knowledge! You have plenty of that.' She looked at

him sharply. 'In a hundred years you get to see a lot of people die. My father. Martha. I know all about you, my Lord.' She drank some tea and put her cup down, her hand shaking slightly.

'I see. And the second thing?' Azrael asked gently. His long fingers caressed the cat as it climbed up to him.

Sarah was silent a long time. Then, abruptly, she stood up.

'It doesn't matter.'

He looked devastated. 'Not still the old family pride, Sarah! I thought you wanted to ask something of me.'

'Maybe I thought better of it,' she muttered.

Tom couldn't bear this. 'She wants you to let her go,' he blurted out. 'Not to . . . take her away.'

'NO!' She glared at him. 'I don't! I'm not going begging to him or anyone! I signed his wretched bargain and I'm going to stick to it.'

Azrael looked upset. He put the cat down and it strolled over to Sarah and butted her knees.

'I'm afraid Sarah's right. The bargain was made, the time has been given and now it must be paid for. Even if I wanted to change things I couldn't, Tom, because even I am bound in the web of the Great Work. I must take a soul with me at the year's end. And it seems Sarah, like her grandfather, would rather die than break her word.'

He stood, gravely. 'And now I'm afraid I have to go. I'm going home for Christmas.'

'To your other estate,' Sarah said coldly.

'Yes.'

'It can't be far.'

He shook his head. 'No. It isn't.'

Disgusted, she stalked to the door and slammed out.

155

She was already running down the stairs when Azrael said, 'After Christmas, Tom, we'll need to work harder. To create a shining new element from all our old mistakes.'

'Don't you care about her?' Tom stared at him in anger. 'She's scared! Why can't you leave her in peace!'

He got to the door before Azrael answered. 'Because I gave her what she most wanted. What is it you want most, Tom?'

He didn't want to say it. But the words came out, hoarse and stumbling.

'To come to this school.'

Azrael nodded. 'It can be arranged,' he said.

Tom turned. It took him a moment to gather the strength to say it. 'I can do it myself.'

Outside the Hall there was no sign of Sarah, and even the slowest of the Waits were far down the drive, the distant brass chords of 'Hark the Herald Angels' drifting faintly back to him. Behind, the Hall was silent.

He was drawn and tired, as if after some struggle. He didn't want to be here alone, in this emptied place, so he ran hurriedly after the singers, knowing they'd go to the church first, then along the cliff and out to the Black Dog. They wouldn't be back much before midnight. Sarah was with them. He needed to talk to her.

Ahead, the lanterns disappeared round the corner.

And as he ran past the thicket of conifers a shadow jumped out and collided with him, hard.

Tom staggered back and almost fell.

Steve Tate hauled him up. 'Right, Tommy,' he hissed, 'now they're all gone you can show me where the money's kept in your posh little school.'

Tom swallowed. 'I can't get back in,' he gasped. His heart was thudding, his palms slippery with sweat. 'It's locked.'

'No problem.' Steve smiled coyly and held up a small key that glittered in the starlight.

'Just look what I've got.'

TWENTY-ONE

'Is this it?'

Steve prowled round the secretary's office in disgust, tugging out the few unopened drawers and flinging them down. 'Where's the cash?'

'I told you! They don't leave money here in the holidays.' Tom shoved a drawer back, terrified. 'Scrab might be round. We should go!'

Steve gave him a glare. 'No chance!' He came round the desk and grabbed Tom's arm, close. Tom struggled.

'Maybe we should try upstairs, eh? All those well-heeled little kiddies' goodies. Come on!'

He was out of the office and racing up the great stairs two at a time; Tom hurtled after him in panic, past the Christmas tree, desperate for Simon to come, or even Scrab. 'Where are you?' his mind thumped, over and over. For an instant outside the staffroom he thought Simon was there, but it was only his own reflection in a thin mirror, and Steve was already inside, rummaging in desks and cupboards, grabbing a screwdriver and wrenching open the grey metal lockers.

'Don't!' Tom hissed, appalled. 'It's just school stuff. Papers. There's nothing valuable here.'

'Rubbish!' Another locker clanged back.

Tom took a step towards the door.

'You stay put!' Steve swung round with the screwdriver in his hand. Quickly he swept the shelves clear; exercise books and folders of notes came down in a waterfall of paper. He kicked them in disgust. Tom turned and fled. He got as far as the door, before the crash of the screwdriver sliced his ear and splintered a chunk out of the doorframe. Then he had the door open, but Steve had grabbed his hair; his head was yanked back, eye-wateringly hard.

'Don't think about turning me in.' The voice was cold and quiet in his ear. 'Or I'll tell them it was you had the key copied. And all about your squatter girlfriend.'

Tom breathed out, a shuddering effort. Steve loosened his grip a fraction.

'So then. Where are the computers?'

'You can't take them.' Tom tried to shake his head; the vicious jerk brought his chin up and water into his eyes. 'They're all marked,' he hissed. 'They'd be traced.'

'I know people.'

Tom didn't believe him. Suddenly, Steve let him go, then shoved his face hard into the door. 'Show me!'

Pain burst like a star in his forehead; his lip felt bruised and cut. Holding it, desperate for Simon, Tom stumbled down the dark corridors. There were few lights on up here; the Hall was deserted, a dim icy place, with only the cold disdain of the Trevelyans in their dusty ruffs and gowns. Tom tripped on a mat, and thought suddenly of the Waits, roaring out 'God Rest Ye Merry, Gentlemen' at some pub. Was Simon with them? Was Simon even real?

Behind him, Steve said, 'What about here?'

It was the door to the Library wing.

Tom's heart thudded. 'No. There's nothing . . .'

But Steve had flung the door open and shoved him in,

and was already flitting from room to room, picking up books and hurling them away in fury. 'Books! Nothing but bloody paper in this place. What's in here?'

It was the Lab.

Tom picked himself up and shrugged, praying that Azrael might still be here.

But the room was empty.

A lamp had been left lit, and it gleamed on the astrolabe and bizarre contraptions of glass, the tubes, one still bubbling, the stacked crucibles and open pages of Azrael's alchemic books.

'More junk.' Steve ran his hand down the telescope, then headed directly for the computer. 'This is better. State of the art!'

He unplugged it, greedily. 'I'll take this. You carry the monitor.' The thought of Azrael's precious research being lost sent shivers down Tom's back. Despite himself, he glanced at the wall safe.

Steve saw him. Instantly he dumped the computer and swung his legs over the bench, smashing a crucible and grinding it to powder under his boot. 'What's in there?'

'I don't know.' Tom stood rigid. Sweat prickled his back.

Steve grabbed the handle and yanked it.

The safe opened.

At once, out in the corridor, a board creaked.

Both of them froze, Tom's heart thudding, a point of pain throbbing in his bruised forehead. In the warm room the planets swung on their invisible wires.

The door moved, a fraction. Terrible darkness widened.

Then, into the thousand glass surfaces in the room a small black cat strolled.

'Bloody thing!' Steve breathed out and turned back to the safe. He flung out papers, a parchment that fragmented as it skittered across the floor. Tom darted over and picked it up. 'Be careful! I keep telling you . . .'

He stopped. Steve had the glass dome in both hands.

'For God's sake. Don't touch that.'

'Why not?' He turned it to the light, and swore. Something moved inside, and then in the glimmer of the lamp they saw it was a small red, scuttling thing, its tail raised to sting, deadly and venomous.

'It's a bloody scorpion!' Steve dropped the jar; Tom made a grab at it, clutching it tight to his chest with sticky hands. 'Leave it!' he hissed.

'Too right. What sort of nut-house is this?'

Tom shoved the jar back into the safe, slammed the door and turned his back on it. He dragged in a deep breath and snapped, 'Right. You win. The stuff you want is downstairs. Right down in the cellars. They lock everything up there over the holidays. Cash, jewellery, CD players, you name it. All the boarders' stuff.'

Steve stared at him, incredulous. 'And you can get in?'

'It's just bolts.'

Still wary, Steve approached him. 'Changed your tune, haven't you, Tommy?'

'Maybe I've just made my mind up about things.' Tom turned. 'Come on.'

He ran. He ran because his whole body was hot with excitement, because if he stopped it would all go cold on him, all the sudden intent, the wild plan that had come from nowhere. Simon wasn't coming. He had to sort this mess out himself.

Without looking back he raced down and down, leading Steve's greedy shadow into the darkest recesses of the house, down to the cold kitchens smelling of school dinners, through the sculleries, down the cellar steps, through the double doors at the bottom where the cider casks of the Treveyan's vast banquets had once rolled.

It was cold here. Numbingly cold.

At the farthest end of the last vault was an ancient strong-door, studded with nails. Tom unbolted it and dragged it open, and the dank opening stank of rats and stale beer.

Steve pushed past and stopped. Far down in the dark, echoes rumbled.

'What's that noise?'

'The Darkwater. They say it runs in a chasm under the house.' The reverberation of the water faded, into silence.

After a minute Steve groped round the walls. 'Where's the light?'

'Here.' Tom reached past him. He could do this. He would do it.

'Well, put the bloody thing on!'

It was easy. Tom shoved; Steve gave a yell and pitched forward. There was a clatter of rolling barrels, then Tom had the door slammed shut and was driving the bolts hard across, top and middle and bottom, solid Victorian rods of iron, and all the yelling and beating of hands from inside suddenly muffled to a dull thumping in his head.

Icily calm, he turned and leaned his back against the door, listening. No one else would hear, unless they came down here.

And no one would.

Because it was Christmas.

'Three days,' he said to himself aloud. 'That was what you gave me. You never told anyone where I was. You just watched and laughed. Three days in the Underworld. Three days in Hell.'

Then he went up the stairs slowly, his mind cold and clear. Closing every door after him he went into every room where Steve had been, wiping fingerprints off, replacing books and papers, closing the lockers, plugging Azrael's computer back in.

The cat was still there, watching.

'And you can shut up,' he said.

By the time he got down to the hall and out on to the front drive, it was midnight. His breath crisped in the damp, smoky air, and the chimes of the church clock seemed to hang over the village, the woods and frosty roofs. Everything was silent when they stopped.

Except, far along the road, the Waits were coming back, a ghostly whisper of chatter getting louder, the faint crunch of feet on gravel.

He shouldn't be seen here.

Slipping into the bushes he made a stealthy detour round by the Devil's Quoits, and to his surprise as the moonlight lit them Simon was there, standing by the largest, hands in pockets.

'Look at this,' he said, as Tom came up.

Steve's scrawled name, the white painted letters, had gone. And they hadn't been scrubbed off. They were gone, as completely as if they'd never been there.

'Weird,' Tom said.

Simon looked at him. 'Not as weird as you. What on earth are you going to do with him? He'll kill you!'

'Let him rot,' Tom said fiercely. 'Or give him to Azrael.'

Turning his back he pushed through the laurels and out into the back of the straggle of Waits, and as the band wearily struck up 'The Holly and the Ivy' he saw the Grey Mare cavorting like a skeletal ghost in the moonlight, and his mother, and Sarah.

She was carrying a lantern. He pushed up behind her. 'Listen. Come over to us tomorrow. For Christmas dinner.'

She stared in surprise. 'Where have you been?'

He looked flushed, she thought, and different. For a moment she wasn't sure if it was Tom or Simon, and then she felt a chill of fear. 'Tom, you haven't made any bargains with him, have you?'

'No. I told him I can sort things out for myself.'

She snorted. 'I used to think that.'

'Well I can. Will you come? Christmas?'

Sarah shrugged. She was going to say no, but then her face softened and she laughed. 'It'll be my last. I'd like it to be at the old place.'

TWENTY-TWO

She took a sip of Coke and looked round.

In what had used to be the scullery Tom was stacking dishes; his mother was gossiping on the telephone in the hall. The passage, Martha would have called it. Martha, she thought fondly, would have loved the phone and would have thought this a palace.

'It's changed so much.'

'Has it?' Simon was sprawled under the tree, playing with some electronic gadget. Tom's Christmas present. He looked up, absently. 'How much?'

She looked at the papered walls, central heating, TV, fridge, and laughed. 'You'd never have recognized it. It was cold, dingy, ragged. There was big range in here with a sea-coal fire. Martha wore herself out black-leading it every week. I slept in that corner.' She nodded at the TV where a cartoon blathered unnoticed. 'It was boarded off. My father's room was your kitchen.'

Simon pressed a few buttons. She thought he wasn't listening, but he said, 'What happened to him?'

'He went back to being the great squire.' She snuggled up on the sofa, feeling relaxed for the first time in weeks. 'When he got back into the Hall he tried to forget places like this ever existed. And Azrael was right about him. He was even more proud. If he saw the Hall now he'd be furious with me.'

Simon was silent. The game bleeped, triumphantly.

Tom called out, 'You'll never beat my score.'

'What you said,' Simon muttered. 'About that domed jar. You really saw us in there, all that time ago?'

'Yes. I saw you.'

He put the game down, in its crackle of Christmas paper. 'No one else can see me.' His voice was quiet, almost a whisper. 'Sometimes I think I'm not a separate person at all, as if Tom and I merge . . . and then split again.' He shook his head. 'And there are times I can't remember . . .'

'You'll never guess what's happened!' Paula had put the phone down and come in, her face flushed with sherry and brandy pudding.

'What?' Tom was there at once. He looked anxious, Sarah thought. In fact he'd been edgy all day.

'Steve Tate's run off!' Paula perched unsteadily on the arm of the sofa.

'Run off?' Tom said quietly.

'Well it looks like it. He was supposed to be staying the night with some mate, but when his father woke up this morning there were these huge white letters painted all over the front of the Post Office. STEVE WAS HERE – that sort of thing. You'd think he'd . . . well, anyway, he and his dad had had some sort of row – between you and me I think he helps himself pretty freely from the till. And he never went to the friends'. Never turned up. So no one knows where he is.'

Slowly, Tom came over and stood by Simon, who glanced at him. They were so alike, Sarah thought.

'His dad must be worried stiff,' she said.

'Beside himself. Been phoning everywhere.'

Tom bit a fingernail. 'Has he called the police?'

'And the coastguard.'

Sarah drank the warm Coke. 'Is this the kid at the Post Office? The one . . .'

'Yes.' Tom frowned; she saw his mother knew nothing of how things were. 'Him.'

'He seemed able to take care of himself.'

'Ah, but the cliffs are dangerous. And the old mine shafts.' Paula glanced at Tom, a swift, uneasy look, as if old memories had been opened. Sarah felt awkward. She drained the glass and put it down. 'Well, thanks Paula. It's been a lovely day. I haven't tasted cooking like yours for years.'

Paula laughed. 'Listen to you! You sound like an old woman! Get Sarah's coat, Tom.'

As he went out, looking preoccupied, Sarah took a last look round. The cold shiver of fear that had crossed her soul so often in the last few months was back. She should have been ready for this. To go with Azrael. To die – that was the word and there was no point hiding from it. She'd had enough time to get used to it. But maybe time on its own wasn't enough. Look at Tom. He should seem like a kid. But he didn't. They were the same age.

There was a framed photograph on the table; an old, sepia image. She picked it up, interested.

'My grandmother.' Paula collected the glasses. 'Taken in about 1920.'

It showed a thin, anxious-looking woman in the loose clothes and cloche hat of the time – Sarah remembered them fondly. But there was something about the face that was familiar, and all at once she saw it, her fingers tightening on the frame. The woman's left eye had a squint, so that she didn't look at you directly.

'What was her name?' she breathed.

'Emmeline Rowney.'

Sarah's breath smudged the glass. Emmeline. She had always wondered what had happened to that half-starved, tearful little waif. After a moment she asked, 'Is she still alive?'

'Oh no, love. She'd be over a hundred! She died in London, just after the war.' Paula was watching, curiously. Sarah put the photo down and as she opened her hand to let it go the reflection of the cane scars, still fresh and red, crossed Emmeline's face in the glass.

Tom walked her home. He was quiet the whole way, walking ahead on the narrow cliff path, brushing the gorse bushes. Far out at sea an oil tanker seemed still. The sea was hushed; its pounding and sloshing sounding hollow among the rocks. Above them the twilight was already dusted with stars, the long streak of the Milky Way breathtakingly clear. Sarah stared up at it, her breath misty.

'She did more than me.'

'Who?'

'Emmeline. She grew up. Scrawny little Emmeline.'

He wasn't listening, twisting gorse spines off in his gloves. 'Sarah . . .'

She pushed past, climbing the stile.

There was something he wanted to say, but it was probably sympathy and she didn't want it. 'What?' she asked, cold.

He shrugged, after a second. 'Nothing.'

On the top of Newhaven Cove they crossed the plank bridge over the tiny Darkwater. Below, in the shadows of the rocks, a small red spark of fire burned. The tramp's fire.

Sarah glared down at it. 'Scrawny little Emmeline,' she muttered to herself.

He said goodnight to her at the front door of the Hall and waited in the shadows, hearing her climb the stairs. A light went on, then off. When he was sure Darkwater was silent he let himself in and crept down to the vaults.

As he came down the passage to the strongroom door a great terror seized him – maybe the door was open and Steve was waiting. But it wasn't. It was just as he had left it, and that terrified him even more. He stood there, not touching it. The passage was lit by only one weak bulb, his breath condensed on the glistening stone walls, the bronze nails. It was bitterly cold. As cold as the mineshaft.

'You should have brought him some food.' Simon leaned accusingly against the wall, arms folded, wearing the jumper Tom had wanted for Christmas but hadn't got.

'He never brought me any. Never came near.'

'Maybe he was scared. He may have thought you were dead.'

Tom snorted. 'Him!'

'And maybe you're scared of the same thing.'

'Rubbish!' Tom put his ear against the door. He heard nothing.

'He'll be frozen.'

'Tough.'

'What if he IS dead, Tom?'

'It never hurt you.'

Simon didn't laugh. 'Grow up. You can't just leave him there.'

'Yes I can.'

Maybe he said it aloud, because there was a sudden faint scrabble at the door.

A whisper came through it. 'Tom? Is that you Tommy? Let me out, Tom, for God's sake! Please, Tommy please let me out!'

It terrified him, gave him a perverse, bitter pleasure. He turned and ran, back up the cellar steps. Simon was waiting at the top.

'Who are you?' Tom yelled. 'My conscience? He's put me through Hell for years – you know that! Scared to go through the village in case he's there, mocking, sniggering, calling after me in the street. Now let him taste how it feels! Let him lie there in the dark for three days with nothing to eat and no one knowing where he is! Let him lick the damp off the walls! He's got it easy. He isn't even hurt.'

'And then what?' Simon came and grabbed his arm. 'What about when he gets out, when he tells everyone? What about when the police come round? What about Paula?'

'She's who I'm thinking of!' Tom shoved past into the kitchens. 'All she went through that time. He did that to her.'

'It's stupid!' Simon raced after him. 'It's not for her, it's for you. And this plan! What makes you think Sarah would ever . . .'

Tom whirled. 'She won't know. And you won't tell her.'

'Me?' Simon yelled at his back as he stalked away. 'I'm dead, remember!'

He didn't want to hear. Racing down the drive under the dark trees he kept his mind off it as though it was a hot thought, a fire that would burn him. Christmas Day had seemed endless, drained of joy. All the time he'd been opening presents, eating, laughing, watching TV, it had all been poisoned by the thought of Steve in the cellar, freezing. It should have been a good thought, but it wasn't. It was hateful. And worst of all, he didn't know how to end it. How could he let Steve out now?

He climbed down the cliff path in the dark. At the bottom the tramp sat up waiting for him, he and the dog both in an old sleeping bag.

'Well,' he said, wriggling back against the cliff face. 'Tha's started some'at, that's for sure.'

'You know?' Tom crouched over the flames, their redness and crackle.

'Searchers.' The tramp grinned. 'Late afternoon till dark; all along the cliffs and coves. In shore lifeboat. Tomorrow, they said, the helicopter. Lines of men beating the cliffs. God, laddie, tha knows how to take revenge.'

'It's not revenge.'

The tramp just wheezed. 'Good luck to thee I say. He's tormented thee, hasn't he?'

Tom sat down. 'Yes,' he said.

'For years he's humiliated thee. He's made thee feel that small . . .'

'He always picks on me.' Tom's fingers gripped. 'I don't know why. I've never done anything to him. Ever!'

'Well now thou has and he's seen tha won't stand for it.' The tramp coughed. Then he looked sideways out of his one eye through the smoke. 'For Azrael, is he?'

'Yes,' Tom said instantly.

171

The tramp grinned, showing black teeth. 'Now you're strong. Feels good, don't it. You've faced up to him. You've . . .'

'But maybe I should take him some food.'

The tramp spat in disgust. 'What! He never.'

'I know.' He looked up. 'But it's December. It's colder than when I fell.'

'Pushed. He pushed thee. And he's indoors.'

'But if he dies.'

The tramp leaned over. Close up he smelt of beer and sweat; his hands were calloused as he grabbed Tom's wrist. 'Listen to me, lad. Don't go soft now. Three days. Leave him there. That's what he deserves. You didn't die.'

Tom pulled away. 'I had Simon.'

'Aye,' the tramp laughed sourly. 'But make him pay, lad. Make him respect thee.'

Tom nodded. 'If you think he'll be all right.'

The tramp spat. 'That sort always are.'

'Tom?'

They both turned, instantly.

Azrael must have come along the cliff-path. He stood halfway down the steps, a shadow in the dimness, and as the tramp and he looked at each other only the hush of the sea moved between them. Then the tramp stood, the sleeping bag kicked away.

'Come here, Tom,' Azrael said.

Tom took a step, then stopped.

Neither of them were looking at him. The tramp stubbed his cigarette out on a rock. 'Tha's looking well, old comrade,' he said, quietly.

Azrael didn't smile. 'Always, you come back. Creating evil.'

'Just passing. Seein' a few friends.'

The firelight crackled, spitting a shower of sparks. 'But don't fret thyself.' The tramp winked. 'I'll take care of these lads.'

'Listen to me.' Azrael's voice was low, a harsh coldness that made Tom look at him in surprise. 'Leave here. Before I compel you.'

The tramp shrugged. 'It'll likely come to that. But tha knows me, old comrade. Thee and I, we were the same once, aeons ago, before they cast me out, those high masters of thine. Such a fall as that was, Azrael! A fall that has no ending, down and down and still I feel myself plummeting eternally, and there's no end to it, because tha falls into thyself and there's no end but death. And for us, old friend, that way out's forbidden.'

'You were the best of us,' Azrael said. 'You turned away.'

'They rejected me. And now I'm the matter thou'll never transmute. I'll not leave what I've begun. In all thy Great Work there's a flaw, and that flaw is me.'

Azrael glanced at Tom. Flamelight flickered over his face; it made him look unhappy. Almost as if he suffered some unbearable sorrow. But all he said was, 'Be careful, Tom. Don't make any arrangements with him. Don't trust him!'

Suddenly Tom felt tired. He couldn't think. He pushed past Azrael and pulled himself up to the cliff path. 'I'm going to bed.'

Below him, the tramp laughed and turned away into the dark. 'That's telling us,' he muttered.

TWENTY-THREE

Scuffles outside Sarah's door woke her; before she could jump out of bed and hide, a key rattled in the lock. Scrab came in sideways and dumped a breakfast tray on the table. He yanked the window curtains wide.

'Always fetching and carrying for you! Thought this set-up would be different.'

'Hello, Scrab,' she said.

His small eyes peered at her as she huddled in the quilt. '' Imself said the condemned woman should eat a decent breakfast. Daft beggar.'

He scratched, scattered a little dandruff, and scraped out. Sarah lay back on the pillow. After a while she managed a relieved smile. Her fate was all worked out. Why worry.

She forced herself to eat some toast, then dressed and went down. Darkwater Hall felt cold and deserted. All its pupils were at home now, having their warm Boxing Days, eating leftover turkey and watching TV. Quite suddenly, gazing up at the Trevelyan portraits on the stairs, she felt like a ghost, left over from an earlier age. She wanted to go home. But this was home.

She took the tray to the kitchens and stacked the dishes in the sink. It was completely silent down here. Except that deep below, something thumped.

She turned the cold tap off and listened.

There it was again.

174

In all her nightly prowls, in all the years she had lived here before, she'd never found the way back to Azrael's mysterious stairway. She'd even had the corridors upstairs peeled open by workmen, but there had been no panel, no door. Had it really been a dream? After all these decades she didn't even know.

She turned, abruptly. The cat was there, and behind it, like a shadow in the doorway, Azrael stood. He had his lab coat on, and there were yellow sulphur stains on his fingers.

'Sarah,' he said quietly, 'there's someone in the cellar.'

She stared.

'Was it your idea? Did the tramp put you up to it?'

'What?'

'Putting him there.'

'I don't know what you're even talking about.' She had rarely seen him so grave.

'Then come on,' he said, hurrying out.

She grabbed a knife from the rack and raced after him. 'A burglar?'

Azrael shrugged. 'I sincerely hope so.'

He snapped the lights on and ran down the steps to the cellars, huge shadows flickering behind him on the wall.

'How did you know about the tramp?' she gasped.

He glanced back, dark. 'This time, Sarah, he won't spoil things for us.'

At the bottom it was damp. Sarah had been here often. The corridor stank of drains, old beer casks, mice. No one bothered with it. But as she raced after him she heard the sound again, a weary thump, faint, as if all the hope had drained out of it.

Azrael ran through the vaults to the door at the end, the strong-door. He gripped the rusted top bolt, grinding it back.

'Quick!' he hissed. 'Hurry, Sarah!'

The bottom bolt was warped; she had to work it frantically up and down before it would shift. Someone had jammed it hard. The thump came again. Just over her head.

'They're locked in!' she gasped.

'I know.'

'But who . . . ?'

'Never mind! Have you got it?'

'Yes!'

The bolt slammed back. Azrael hauled the door wide. A pitiful figure, filthy with dust, tearstained, bloodstained, collapsed into his arms.

Scrab opened the front door so suddenly that Tom almost put the key into his eye.

'Oh my Gawd. Yer for it.'

'What?'

Scrab grinned and stood aside. Coming in, Tom saw the Christmas tree in the hall had been lit up again, towering in its green height against the stair-rail.

'And 'aven't we been a wicked little boy!' Scrab slammed the door; Tom almost jumped.

'I don't know what you're talking about.'

The caretaker laid a dirty finger along his nose and tapped it. 'Saying nowt. But 'Imself's upstairs. High and mighty today, so I wouldn't keep 'im waiting. Always like this, after 'e's been 'obnobbing with the Powers that Be.'

Uneasy, Tom took the stairs two at a time and walked

boldly into the library, his whole body listening for sounds from below. But the only thudding was his heart. He wondered what was coming.

The Lab was gloomy.

Azrael was leaning against the fireplace on one elbow, watching him. To his surprise Sarah was there too. As soon as she saw him she leapt up. 'You stupid, stupid fool,' she snapped.

'What?' Tom stopped dead. Simon came in behind him, reflected grotesquely in twisted tubing. 'What have I done?'

'You know!' She seemed too angry for words.

Of course he knew.

They had found Steve.

Tom rubbed his face nervously. 'Look. You don't understand . . .'

'I know what's been going on! But do you think doing it back to him will help?'

Azrael's silence was terrifying. Tom turned to him. 'Is he alive?'

'Alive!' Azrael's voice was airy and dangerous. 'That's such an interesting word, don't you think, Tom? What does it mean, to be alive? Do you have to be born, to be alive?'

He paced under the spinning planets. 'Are only the sons of men alive? Or are there different sorts of life, different deepnesses of being? Angels and demons?'

'Azrael . . .' Sarah said shortly.

'Maybe in a way that boy was not alive before. Not alive to the suffering he caused you.'

Tom shook his head. 'Please. Tell me.'

Azrael put both hands down on the bench and leaned

over. 'There is no place for revenge, Tom, in the Great Work. It's a corruption in the crucible, a gritty unburning cinder. You should never have done this.'

His anger was bleak, a darkness in the room. All his geniality was gone, this was a new being, relentless, unknown.

'Stop tormenting him,' Sarah muttered.

The alchemist turned in disgust. 'He's alive. There. No thanks to you.'

The domed jar was on the bench. Tom bent over it, rubbing a hole in the dust. Cobwebs brushed his eyelashes as he gazed in.

Steve Tate lay on a white bed. He was still, as if asleep, and tiny – so tiny Tom could have picked him up with finger and thumb. His face was filthy, his hands bandaged, as if he had banged and scraped for hours on door and walls. He looked exhausted and half starved. Pitiful.

Tom should have felt glad. But he didn't.

'And the worst thing was,' Azrael's voice said behind him, 'that you planned to offer this soul to me.'

Tom closed his eyes.

'And if you think,' Sarah stalked up and down in utter contempt, 'that I would ever let anyone take my place . . .'

'You weren't supposed to know.'

Azrael came and covered the jar with a black velvet cloth. He turned. 'Who's idea was this?'

'Mine.'

'Not entirely. Someone else suggested it.' He stepped closer. 'I think I know who.'

'No.'

'Tell me, Tom.'

Tom was stubbornly silent. Simon's voice startled them all.

'The tramp put him up to it.'

Azrael looked straight at him. To Tom's astonishment he nodded, curtly. 'As I thought. SCRAB!'

He yelled it; instantly the door flew open and Scrab sloped in, a dark coat slung over one arm.

' 'Eard it all.' He held the coat up; Azrael flung it on and was gone, sweeping through the Library, all the book pages ruffling in his draught, the papers flying.

Tom looked at Sarah in terror. 'What will he do to him?'

She looked uneasy. 'I never saw, last time. But they're enemies, Tom, all down the centuries.'

Doors banged below.

Running down the stairs they found the house was crackling into life, shadows gathering, the corridors full of footsteps, the slavering of hounds. Azrael leapt the last step, coat flying.

'Stay here!' he yelled over his shoulder. 'Don't let them out, Scrab.'

Breathless, the caretaker shuffled behind. 'Still giving yer blasted orders,' he muttered.

Out of the rooms, the cupboards, the desks, a host of presences gathered, invisibly slipping past on the stairs, a running emptiness. Sarah grabbed Tom. 'Quick!'

They had to push their way through; the air hummed and jostled with the whisper and crackle of beings they couldn't see. *Powers and principalities*, Tom found himself whispering. *Angels and demons*.

'OY! You get back 'ere!'

Scrab was screeching, but they were out, and the grey

afternoon was agitated by sudden wind, and out to sea a storm cloud was looming down on them, terrifyingly black, its underside lit by electric glimmers.

'There he is!' Simon yelled.

Azrael was a fleet shape among the trees; they struggled after him. Huge drops of rain fell, icy, the wind buffeting them back.

'What do you mean, down the centuries?' Tom gasped.

'Never read your Bible?' Sarah thrust fir branches aside. 'There was a war in heaven, remember.' Then she hissed, 'The Quoits! That's where he's going!'

As he ran Tom felt Simon close; the sleet swirled down, freezing into flakes that soaked his coat and Sarah's jumper, and he saw that they soaked Simon too. Tiny flakes, like white feathers, that stuck to his lips and stung like acid. Simon grabbed him.

'Look at me! I'm cold!'

He seemed elated, holding his arms up to it, hair plastered to his neck, drops running down his face. 'I can feel it, Tom! I can feel the snow!'

'It's like no snow I know,' Sarah muttered.

Nor was it. It was a storm of shards and slivers; it stabbed and stung, and the trees roared under it, even the muddy soil seeming to boil, and for an instant Tom was convinced they were running through the bubble and hiss of some vast cosmic experiment, until he crashed against the wet bark of a tree, and saw the Quoits.

The black stones streamed with frost.

His back flat against the nearest stone, the tramp stood, facing them. He had drawn himself up, and now he flung his arms open and laughed.

'So tha's come for me, Azrael! What good will it do thee, old friend?'

Lightning glimmered.

Among the dark trees, Azrael was barely visible. All around him the sleet hissed and the wood crackled with movement.

'I warned you,' he whispered.

A hound's tongue licked Tom's hand; he jerked back in terror. Close around his knees the darkness panted and pressed.

'Have I maimed thy work again?' the tramp said cheerily. 'Well I'm sorry, lad. But tha knows me. Only I can follow thee down the twelve stairways, and I will. I'll face thee in all the world's ages.'

The tramp dropped his arms. Rain dripped from his coat hem. 'It's hard for thee,' he muttered. 'All else is thine, but not me, eh? Not till the end itself. Tha'll never be free of me.'

Thunder rumbled, a hollow grumble. Azrael said clearly 'Come back to us.'

The tramp spread his hands. 'Too late. I've changed.'

'You can be as you were.'

The tramp laughed. 'Aye? But I don't want to.'

For a moment Azrael was silent. Then he raised his face, the rain dripping from his hair. 'I'm sorry, brother,' he whispered.

Lightning cracked. A spear of it. It shot through the hand Azrael held up, and in one vivid instant the tramp was there, pinned to the stone with sheer light and a scream that shocked Tom rigid. An implosion of rock stung him; he was flung back into a wet hollow of dripping brambles, all the night seared with a horrifying, scorching smell. Dizzy, lifting his head, he saw a darkness slither away between the stones.

Snow fell, silent. Beside him Sarah scrambled up, blood running from a cut on her forehead; Simon looked stunned.

'Did you see?' he whispered. 'He killed him.'

'You can't kill evil,' Sarah said.

Only the sleet pattered, and around them, for miles, the wood was empty.

Azrael lowered his hand, turned and saw them. He pulled his coat tighter and strode past them. His voice was bleak and weary.

'I told you to stay inside,' he snarled.

TWENTY-FOUR

Days passed.

On the 27th, Steve Tate was found wandering on the beach at Padstow, suffering, Paula said drily, from amnesia. Nothing seemed to be wrong with him, but he had no idea where he'd been.

Tom listened, staring out of the window at the sea. He was surprised to find he didn't care.

On the 28th and 29th it rained. He kept away from the Hall; the memory of Sarah's anger was terrible.

On the 30th he ventured out, tormented. Below the cliff the tramp's encampment was empty, the sleeping bag sodden, the dog gone. The middle one of the Devil's Quoits had a hole burned right through it, as if with a powerful laser. A rainbow pool of some oily stuff stank at its base.

He couldn't stand it any longer. He crept into the Hall and up to her room, but she'd locked herself in and wouldn't open the door.

'Get lost and leave me alone!' she yelled at last.

'Sarah, please! Never mind about me. You saw what he did to the tramp. Is that what he'll do to you? You've got to make some effort to escape at least!'

No answer.

Then Scrab came muttering down the corridor and Tom slid, shadowy, down the stairs.

He kept away from Azrael.

Finally, it was the 31st.

The last day.

All morning he felt confused and sick. Azrael seemed so gentle. But the tramp was dead. He felt cold even thinking about it.

'I don't see why you won't come.' Behind him, his mother buttoned her coat.

Tom picked up the remote control. 'There's a film I want to see.'

'Please yourself.' She checked her purse and unlatched the door. 'I'll be back about ten. For New Year.'

He didn't switch the TV on, couldn't stand all that fake jollity. He didn't know how long he'd stared at the blank screen or even what he was thinking, when the door opened again.

'Tom.'

It was Sarah. And Simon.

She was pale, warmly dressed, with the rucksack, her hair scraped back into a blue elastic. 'I can't go through with it,' she muttered.

He jumped up. 'What?'

'I've tried, but I can't. I've got to do something! Even if you think I'm a coward, I'm going to run, Tom. If Azrael wants me he's got a hunt on. Maybe he's not as powerful as I thought. Maybe I can get away. Anywhere. I can't stand waiting any more.'

Tom grabbed his coat. 'You're not a coward. And I'm coming.'

'That's what I said.' Simon had been missing for days. Now he seemed thinner, his tired face drawn.

'Where is Azrael?'

Tom shrugged into his coat.

184

'In the Lab. Night and day. It's a furnace in there, everything bubbling, dripping. Scrab's taking food in; says 'Imself's so close to success he can't sit still for excitement.' She shrugged, wan. 'So now's my chance.'

'Right.' Tom crammed some chocolates from the tree into his pocket. 'We go over the cliffs to Marazy Head, then cross the moor. At the main road we'll hitch a lift to Bodmin, and you can get a train.'

'It's New Year's Eve!'

'Then we'll hurry! They'll run till about eleven. Come on, Sarah!'

She ran a hand through her hair; it was dark at the roots. 'Lead on, Hero.'

They ran down the lane and across the caravan field. There was no way to avoid the village; Tom saw Steve's dad up a ladder scrubbing the white letters angrily off the Post Office.

All across the cliffs they kept to the footpath, the stiff brown umbels of summer hemlock scraping at them. The afternoon was rapidly darkening. Home-going ramblers passed them, with quiet hellos.

At the Darkwater, Sarah stopped.

'Be careful. From upstairs in the house you can see this stretch.'

'Azrael's busy.'

'Scrab isn't. We should cross the beach.'

Without waiting for him to agree she ran down the steps. He and Simon raced after her.

The gulls circled, screaming, their cruel yellow beaks wide. Newhaven was a dimness of salt and seaweed, sand gritty on the steps.

They struggled over the soft sand. The harder ridges

were easy, their footsteps clear across them and Tom saw that even Simon left them now, faint footmarks. At the north cliff they scrambled over fallen rock, sliding on huge banks of slippery bladderwrack, splashing into pools, over limpeted boulders corrugated with barnacles.

Finally Sarah reached the cliff. 'Up here?'

'There's a path.' Tom pushed past. 'This way.'

He'd climbed Star Cliff before but it was tricky; the path slid and shifted year by year. Tides washed it away. Handholds of soft rock stuck out, some with fossils embedded.

Tom hauled himself up. Below, Sarah's boots scraped. Suddenly he felt good, even elated. Tate would never remember, but he did, and it would all be different now. That memory of the tiny tear-stained boy in the jar had changed him. Steve might be as obnoxious as ever, but he, Tom, was already different. Grabbing a handful of wet bracken, he dug his toes in and squirmed up over the crumbling soil.

A hand reached down.

'Come on,' Simon hissed. His brother's grip was wet and firm. And warm.

They hauled Sarah up and crouched, breathless. The sun was almost gone; a redness deep in veils of mist. Inland, over the fields and combes of its estate, Darkwater Hall glowed red. All its facade burned, warm light lapping it, every window a blaze of flame. For a second Tom thought it really was on fire, but the sun sank and night enveloped the house, dimming it to a dark hulk against the purple sky.

Crossing the moor was a nightmare.

Threads of path were too easy to lose, the ground

boggy and tremulous. The light was almost gone. Simon led them, Tom stumbling last, twice plunging his boots into water over the ankle, so his feet were soaked and squelching.

It grew so dark he could barely see. Gnarled shadows of windbent trees rose up like claws; distant tors were bizarre shapes of toppling rock. Towards Bodmin the sky glowed with streetlights.

It was Tom who stopped and looked back.

For a second he had heard it clearly; a sound that froze him.

The snuffle and pad of a hound.

Or was it the wind, the dead bracken hissing?

'Come on!' Sarah yelled.

He ran after them. This was Temple Combe, a ravine that plummeted between bushes and a stand of trees, dark firs, rare on the moor. In their pitch blackness he ran right into Sarah before he saw her.

'What's wrong?' Her voice was a whisper.

He glanced back. 'I thought I heard something.'

In the silence the branches sissed, an eternal sound. The snuffle, or whatever it was, would be lost under them.

Wordless, Sarah pulled him on. They walked into blindness, their only guide the puddles on the track; ghostly echoes of the lighter sky. Ahead, as they slipped and skidded down, the track turned a corner. Eerie sounds came towards them, voices wailing, far across the moor.

Heart thudding, Sarah stopped.

They listened, under the pine smell of the branches.

'It's a black dog all right,' Tom said in relief. 'But not that sort.'

At the pub, when they reached it, the New Year revels had started. The windows spilled warm light; the car park was lit with multicoloured lanterns.

Sarah walked past quickly, clutching the stitch in her side; Tom followed, till the well-known voice stopped him rigid.

'Tommy! Look lads, it's lover boy!'

After a second, he turned.

Steve Tate was sitting on the doorstep with a can of beer in his hand. He crushed it now; the metal crumpled with a loud crack. The other two, Mark and Rob, came out of the pub.

'Come on,' Sarah said uneasily.

Tom didn't hesitate. As he marched straight up to them Steve scrambled to his feet; even before Tom grabbed his collar there was a startled disbelief in his face.

'I never liked that name,' Tom said pleasantly. 'I don't want to hear it again. OK?'

Steve tried to pull back; Tom gripped tighter.

'What's got into you?'

'I pushed you into a cellar and slammed the door on you,' Tom said quietly. 'And I saw what it did to you.'

For a second Steve was still; then he wrenched away and laughed a startlingly false laugh. 'You're a bloody nutcase.'

Tom turned away.

'Happy New Year,' he said, over his shoulder.

Sarah had her arms folded; Simon was grinning. They swung into step beside him.

'Well,' she said, 'I'm impressed. But he'll be furious.'

Tom glanced back. Steve was yelling at Mark, flinging the beer can at him. 'He won't change. But I have.'

'They might come after you.'

'I don't care.' The strange thing was, it was true.

Sarah opened the farm gate. 'So maybe Azrael was wrong and the tramp was right. There is a place for revenge.'

'I should have been able to do it without all that.' He slipped through after her, jarring rows of hanging drops from the gate-bar.

Far off, Mamble church clock chimed; they counted, silent. Eight.

Four hours to midnight.

Now they ran hard. Down Branscombe, spattering the mud at the bottom, into the black, empty stretch of moor towards Stee. This was treacherous ground. Faint steams and wisps of fog rose from it, gathering in hollows.

And then, close behind, the dog howled.

Tom turned. They waited, a breathless hush. To their left another howl, nearer.

'They're out,' Sarah said grimly. 'He's hunting me.'

Dark shapes loped and slithered.

'Water!' Tom caught her hand and they splashed into the bog, sinking instantly, Simon behind them. Floundering, they struggled in the cold to keep their footing, stumbling on buried tussocks.

The howls were nearer. All around them now the midnight hounds slavered and ran. Tom glanced back. 'Keep up,' he called, anxiously.

Simon's face was a paleness in the mist. He slipped, and yelled. Tom let go of Sarah's arm and swore. 'I'll have to go back for him!'

'Wait!' she gasped, but even as she said it a rapid barking rang out; Simon was swallowed in the clinging fog. Only his voice screamed, terrifed and in agony. 'Tom! It's got me! TOM!'

Tom didn't hesitate. 'Go on!' he yelled. Floundering back he burst through the fog into a knot of darkness. Hounds flew apart; one backed slowly, head down, growling. But the other held its grip, and to his amazement he saw it had hold of Simon's arm and was pulling him down. He had fallen on his knees in the marsh, struggling and swearing, clothes sopping with water. He looked terrified.

And his arm was bleeding.

TWENTY-FIVE

'Tom!' His brother grabbed, sank.

Tom kicked at the hound, hard in its chest. The growl simmered in its throat.

'It's hurting me!'

'I know! Wait!'

'Here!' Sarah was there; she dragged a broken gorse branch in one hand and a heavy stick in the other. She threw the stick; he grabbed it before it sank and thwacked the bog furiously. Mud and water flew up; algae spattered everything.

'Get out!' he yelled. 'Go on! Go on!'

The hound opened its teeth and barked.

With a gasp of relief Simon fell backwards; Sarah grabbed him, pulling him up.

'Get him away!' Tom yelled. He backed, cautiously. All around in the fog the slinking shapes circled, their paws deep in the evil-smelling murk. For a moment as Sarah and Simon splashed into darkness he thought the whole pack would rush at him, their small red eyes blinking like coals. He gripped the stick, planted his feet firmly.

'So come on,' he breathed.

At once, far off, a low whistle echoed.

The pack melted.

In seconds the fog was empty.

After a while, he turned and struggled on. The ground

grew more solid; the legs of his trousers stuck to him in the sudden bitter cold.

'Where are you?' he called.

'Over here.'

In the shelter of a stone wall Sarah had Simon's sleeve rolled up and was mopping the bite with something. Blood ran freely down his wrist. They all stared at it, fascinated.

'What's happening to me?' Simon whispered.

Tom shook his head. 'Can you stop it?'

'I can tie it up.' Sarah's wet fingers worked fast. 'That's about all.' She grinned at Simon. 'Does it sting?'

'It's throbbing like mad,' he said gloomily.

Tom laughed. 'Welcome to the human race. But let's go. Before those creatures come back.'

The fog confused them. There were no stars to see, and the moor seemed endless on each side; they struggled on for almost an hour until Tom knew they were lost. They should have reached the main road a long time ago.

'In this light we won't see it till we get right up to it,' Sarah gasped. 'There'll be no traffic.'

And no lift either, Tom thought, but he said nothing. Pausing for breath in the lee of a thorn bush, he listened.

Over the blackness of the moor came a new sound. A whine, high, almost unhearable. Machinery.

'Listen!'

They kept still, Simon crouched breathless on his heels. 'What is it?'

'It's over that way.' Tom looked into the fog.

'What if that's the wrong way?' Simon muttered.

'It's as good as any other.' In the darkness Tom wiped water off his watch and held it close to his eyes. 'Nine forty.' He went and tugged his brother gently to his feet. 'Come on. We'll get there.'

'I've got a pain in my side, I'm cold, wet and scared.' Simon rubbed his face ruefully. 'If this is being alive, you can keep it.'

'Oh I don't know.' Sarah pushed ahead of him grimly. 'It seems pretty good to me.'

The sound was coming from a fluorescent light fixed under the rickety forecourt of a garage. In the foggy air the light crackled and hummed. A radio was playing in the office somewhere; as they crept down the lane towards it a car passed them, going slow.

'Quick!' Tom turned the corner into the forecourt. The car had pulled up for petrol.

'Right,' Tom said. 'You'd better go. Ask for a lift to Bodmin. Then we'll come.'

'Brilliant!' She was sarcastic, but she stepped out.

The car door swung open.

Scrab got out.

Instantly Sarah flattened herself behind one of the petrol pumps.

The round-shouldered man looked impatient. He pulled the petrol hose out, muttering irritably; they could see his overalls under the greasy coat. As the petrol went in he glanced around, small eyes watchful.

In the shadows, not a metre from him, Sarah didn't move.

'He'll see her,' Simon breathed.

It seemed an age before Scrab propped the pipe back. His breath smoked in the foggy air as he searched his pockets for money. Then he crossed the forecourt slowly, opened the shop door and went in.

Sarah ran back. 'We could steal the car,' she breathed.

Tom stared at her. 'I can't drive. Can you?'

'No. But . . .'

'What about him?' Simon hissed.

A lorry driver was coming out. A young man, with a cheeseburger in a box. The smell of it was torture. They caught him at his cab.

'Any chance of a lift?' Sarah said quickly.

He stared at her. 'Both of you? Where you heading?'

'Bodmin station.'

'Bit out of my way.' He opened the cab door. Tom glanced back anxiously at the lit garage shop. Scrab was counting coins out of a leather purse, reluctantly.

'Not eloping, are you?' the driver grinned.

Sarah fixed him with a desperate stare. 'Look it's really important. I HAVE to get the last train! We'll miss it otherwise. Oh please! It is New Year.'

He climbed up, put the box on the dashboard and looked down at them. Then he said, 'Get in.'

They tore round and scrambled up into the cabin. On the radio Big Ben struck ten.

Scrab came out.

Tom slammed the door; the caretaker looked up, instantly alert. For a second their eyes met in the driving mirror.

Then the lorry roared away.

The driver ate the cheeseburger with one hand, the cab loud with country and western music. It was warm and muggy; Tom almost relaxed until the driver swallowed his last mouthful and said, 'Bloody maniac.'

'Who?'

'Him, behind us. In the Beetle.'

Scrab's car had caught up fast. Now it careered across the lane from hedge to hedge, tooting, flashing its lights.

194

'Maybe I'd better pull over.'

'No!' Sarah said quickly. 'Please! I'll miss the train.'

The driver wiped his mouth and threw down the tissue. 'Seems to me ma'am,' he drawled, his voice suddenly mock-American, 'that there varmint's after yous.'

They glanced at each other. 'Sort of.'

'Lookee here, are you all . . .'

'We're not running away.' Sarah turned to him. 'I'm going home. He's some . . . nutcase. I can't explain. He wants to try and stop me, and I'm really scared.'

She did it well, Tom thought. The driver almost swelled to John Wayne before their eyes. He changed gear, noisily. 'OK pardners. You want him lost. I'll lose him.'

Hedges loomed, black in the headlights. Shadows flickered across the lane. They roared along, the load in the back crashing, taking bends crazily. When they reached the main road across the moor it was deserted; they squealed on to it on two wheels, and then the driver slammed his foot down.

'Come on punk!' he yelled. 'Make my day!' And then, suddenly 'YEE-HAR!'

They hit ninety on the straight. At every bend Tom closed his eyes and prayed, but Simon leaned out of the window and whooped and yelled. 'We're losing him! He's miles back!'

The Beetle was tiny in the darkness. The dashboard clock said 10.10.

'What time's this here train, ma'am?'

'Ten thirty,' Sarah shouted.

'No problemo!'

They sped around the roundabout, the driver singing 'Clementine' at the top of his voice. He already wore a red neckerchief and checked shirt; now he fished a cowboy's hat from under his seat and crammed it on.

'We'll get you to the fort, ma'am, before them pesky redskins shoot us down. Nobody stops a Wells Fargo coach!'

Sarah giggled.

Tom felt sick.

In Bodmin the doors of the pubs were open; the streets busy with people. The lorry had to slow. A red light stopped them. Sweating, Tom stared at the mirror. Far back, the Beetle came round a corner.

The lights changed. They roared down the street, right, left, down the lanes, wildly into the station entrance. Flinging the door wide Tom tumbled out, Sarah grabbed her bag and planted a kiss on the driver's forehead. 'Happy New Year, pardner.'

Then they were running.

The ticket office was shut, but the roaring as they ran by it told them a train was coming, the London express by the noise. It thundered through, filling the night with vibrations and oil-stink, and as they flung themselves down the last stairs it pulled up alongside and braked, sleek and dark in a cloud of frosty steam.

'Yee-har!' Simon whooped.

Sarah raced along the platform. 'You've been brilliant,' she yelled turning. 'I'll write!'

The engine screeched to a deafening halt. Doors opened. She grabbed the nearest handle, yanked it round.

A passenger stepped out. A tall man, in a long black coat. He stood on the frosty platform and smiled ruefully at her.

'I'm sorry, Sarah,' he said.

TWENTY-SIX

Scrab drove them home.

For most of the way no one spoke. Azrael lounged in the back with Tom and Simon; Sarah sat in front, grimly clutching her rucksack. Sickening disappointment numbed them; they were cold and nauseated with it. The only sound was the car's low purr, and Scrab sucking his teeth or whistling through them cheerfully.

Stone walls gleamed in the headlights. A few drops of rain pattered on the side windows.

Finally, Azrael stirred. 'Well. I did warn you. You could never have escaped from me.'

'It was worth a try!'

He shrugged, unhappy. 'Even after all this time, Sarah, you still don't trust me.' He sounded depressed. 'I find that very hurtful. Have I ever hurt you? Do you really believe that I'm some creature of evil, that I seek anybody's destruction?'

'Only mine.'

Azrael sighed. He rubbed his face with one open palm. 'I'm not evil, Sarah. Evil is stealthy. It whispers and insinuates. It uses fear, turns soul against soul. All I want to do is finish my Great Work. To make gold from dross.'

'Whatever it costs?'

He sat back, morosely. 'It costs everything.'

'I did what you asked, Azrael. I made up for all the

Trevelyans, their oppressions, their greed. I spent a hundred years on it.'

'There is still one Trevelyan you haven't atoned for.'

She glared at him, twisting round. 'Who?'

'Yourself. And you've forgotten this.' He took a piece of paper out of his pocket and held it up. She saw her red signature again, firm and clear. Tom and Simon stared at it curiously. Then Azrael folded it and put it away. 'People always find it so difficult at the end,' he said, sadly.

The car purred up the long drive to Darkwater in silence. They climbed out, stiff and cold, the gravel crunching frostily. Simon held his torn wrist as if it ached. Tom stood by Sarah. No one spoke.

They climbed the steps to the porch and the gargoyles leered down at them, small drips from the lips of one splashing Scrab's head so that he swore.

Azrael took his bunch of keys and unlocked the door, and as they went in he flicked the lights on in the marble hall. One of the clocks in the house chimed gently. It was eleven forty-five.

'This way,' Azrael murmured. To their surprise he didn't climb the stairs to the Library but crossed instead to the small door of the cubby-hole under the landing, half hidden by the vast dark growth of the Christmas tree.

'There?' Sarah sounded disgusted.

Azrael shrugged, opening it. 'Here. The door is always where you least expect it.'

A faint red glow lit the tiny space. Behind hung-up coats and mildewed suitcases they saw a small metal staircase, spiralling down. Sarah flung down her rucksack under the Christmas tree and drew herself up. Then she held out her hand, firmly.

'Goodbye Tom. Thanks for all your help.'

He didn't shake it.

'No. I'm coming.' He glanced at Azrael. 'I want to see.'

The alchemist hesitated. Then he shrugged, elegantly. 'If you wish. Scrab, stay at the back, there's a good fellow.'

He picked up a lantern from a corner and lit it with a small silver lighter. Then he led them down.

At first their feet clattered on the iron stairs, but at some point in the dimness of the descent the steps became stone and the walls, rock. Tom ran his hand down; the surface was wet and warm, with dripping green lichens sprouting through the cracks. It got hotter. He undid his coat, already sweating.

The glow increased. Below him was a redness, and Azrael's faint candle was lost in it, a fiery heat scorching up at them.

'Listen to that!' Simon said in his ear.

The underworld river roared. Far below them it thundered through deep chasms in the rock, and Sarah heard it too, gripping her hands tightly together, not turning her head. Come on, she thought acidly. What use was a hundred years of life if it didn't prepare you for death? She wouldn't tremble, or beg. She'd take it, like she'd taken the five cuts all that endless, impossible time ago. And for a moment she remembered the swish of the cane, the fine strands of hair unpinning from Mrs Hubbard's glossy bun. Maybe pride was good for something after all.

Azrael came to the bottom of the steps and put the lantern down. Turning he helped her round the last corner. She stared.

The caverns were enormous. One out of another they

led deep into steamy distance, and flooding them all was a vast lake of simmering black water, the vapours that rose from its surface condensing on the invisible roof, dripping and plopping from rock to rock like an eternal rain. It was unbearably hot. Half-glimpsed in the steam were fissured tunnels and arches, seamed with crystal and quartz. And far away in the depths of the earth the chasm thundered, the fall of the water deafening, as if it plummeted down circle after circle, weir after weir, into a bottomless pit.

On the shingle was a small boat, painted black, with two oars.

Azrael gave Scrab a nod; the little man spat on his hands, then crunched over and pushed the boat afloat. He clambered in, awkward. 'Come on then. 'Aven't got all day.'

Azrael looked at Sarah. He held out his hand.

She went to take it.

'WAIT!' Tom's hiss echoed. A thousand drips fell. He grabbed her. 'Wait.'

'Tom, it's . . .'

'No.' He turned to Azrael. 'Listen. You want a soul, you can have one. I'll go.'

'You?' Azrael smiled and shook his head. 'I'm sorry Tom, I can't allow that.'

'He doesn't mean him. He means me.'

Simon shouldered between them. He was wet and bedraggled. The dirty handkerchief round his wrist was crusted with dried blood. His clothes were as cheap and scruffy and mud-splattered as Tom's. They had never, Sarah realised, been so alike.

'This is the bargain,' he said quickly. 'You take me,

200

and you leave Sarah. I want that.'

'Well I don't!' Sarah snapped hotly.

'You must!' Simon pulled her away from Azrael's hand. 'Please. I don't want to stay. Maybe it's a journey I should have made years ago.' He turned to Tom. 'Don't you think?'

Tom was appalled. Every part of him wanted to cry out *no*. And yet something had changed. He and Simon. Somehow they had swapped places, become each other. He reached out, gently and took his brother's hand. Then he hugged him close. Over his shoulder he said, 'Yes.'

Azrael was watching carefully. 'Sarah?' he murmured.

She couldn't speak. It took her a long time to say 'I can't.'

Tom stepped back. 'You have to. We're doing it for you.'

'I can't take Simon away from you.'

'It's not that,' Tom said, exasperated. 'You still won't step back, will you? You're still Miss Sarah Trevelyan, far above the rest of us, last of the proud, terrible Trevelyans. Please Sarah. End it all. Let it go.'

She stared at them both, her eyes faintly wet. Then at Azrael. 'Would you agree?'

He folded his arms, his face tense with excitement. 'I would. But you must accept it. You have to say yes. You have to throw away your pride.'

The Darkwater roared. Steam rose. In the boat Scrab fidgeted tetchily. 'For Gawd's sake get yerselves sorted out! Some of us 'ave a life to live.'

'Yes.'

The word was so quiet they barely heard it.

She said it again, firmer, looking at Tom and Simon. 'Thank you. Yes.'

Azrael smiled, joyfully. 'At last! Sarah, I am so delighted!' He kissed her quickly, climbed into the swaying boat and sat down, taking out a small box from his pocket, a snuff box that she recognized as her grandfather's. Azrael opened it, looking pleased, and rather shy.

'The Great Work,' he said, 'is completed.'

A small circle of gold glinted inside.

'You did it!' she gasped.

'WE did it. Despite all the mistakes of the past, all the pride of the Trevelyans, the cruelty, the selfishness. After all the fear, finally, we have something to show.' He took the gold out carefully and held it out to Scrab, whose greedy fingers closed on it quickly. He bit it, nodded, and shoved it in his pocket with a grin of satisfaction.

'Right. Let's be 'aving yer.'

Simon glanced at Tom, climbed down into the boat, and sat. Scrab took the oars, grinding one against the shingle. Slowly, the boat turned.

'Yes, but what happens to me?' Sarah said suddenly.

Azrael sat back. 'From the last stroke of midnight, our bargain is dissolved.'

'Will I turn into dust or something?'

He looked at her, darkly amused. 'You'll grow up, Sarah. What exactly do you think I am?'

'I don't know,' she said quietly. 'I don't think I'll ever know.'

The boat was fading, lost in the mist.

'One day you will,' Azrael's voice said, faintly. 'But goodbye. For now.'

'See you,' Tom whispered. Simon waved, a shadow, then a greyness, then nothing at all. Only the slop of oars came back, a ripple of water.

And the echo of his own voice.

'See you,' it said.

For a long time they stood there, the empty water lapping at their feet.

Outside, on the steps of Darkwater they came out into the cold and counted the chimes from the church. After the twelfth there was a faint burst of cheering. A maroon went up from a boat in the harbour. Fireworks began, popping and whistling and cracking into coloured showers.

'Feel any different?' he asked.

She shrugged. 'No. You?'

'Empty.'

She nodded, looking out at the stars. 'Will you come to this school, Tom?'

'I'll try. I owe Simon that.'

'You'll get in,' she said drily. 'I'll make sure.'

He shrugged. 'Maybe it doesn't matter. I've learned what I needed to. But what will you do?'

She was silent a moment. Finally she said, 'You can tell me where Emmeline's grave is. And then, I'll go to college.'

'I'd have thought you'd have done that already.'

She was rubbing her eyes. A tiny lash came off and lay on the edge of her finger; she stared at it in delight.

'Never been old enough,' she said.